First published in Great Britain in 1965
by Faber and Faber
Republished in 2011 by
Peepal Tree Press Ltd
17 King's Avenue
Leeds LS6 1QS
England

ISBN13: 9781845231644

Supported by
ARTS COUNCIL
ENGLAND

T0160112

ALSO BY WILSON HARRIS

Fiction:
Palace of the Peacock
Far Journey of Oudin
The Whole Armour
The Secret Ladder
Heartland
The Waiting Room
Tumatumari
Ascent to Omai
The Sleepers of Roraima
The Age of the Rainmakers
Black Marsden
Companions of the Day and Night
Da Silva da Silva's Cultivated Wilderness and
  Genesis of the Clowns
The Tree of the Sun
The Angel at the Gate

Poetry:
Fetish
Eternity to Season

THE EYE OF THE SCARECROW

WILSON HARRIS

INTRODUCTION BY MICHAEL MITCHELL

PEEPAL TREE

For Margaret,
Antony and Elizabeth Tasker
and
Mary Wilson

Sightless, unless
The eyes reappear
T.S. ELIOT

CONTENTS

INTRODUCTION

MICHAEL MITCHELL

It was T.S. Eliot who pointed out, in his essay "The Frontiers of Criticism", that the fundamental business of the critic was to promote the understanding and enjoyment of literature.[1] If you have just picked up this novel with the idea that you might read it, or have just finished the novel and are somewhat baffled by it, these few brief introductory remarks have been designed to help you to both enjoy it more and understand it better.

The Eye of the Scarecrow is a frontier novel. By that I don't mean it is about adventure on the edge of empire, or lawlessness beyond the reaches of metropolitan power, but about a far more radical approach to geographical, cultural, psychological and metaphysical frontiers, as well as frontiers of literary form. When people say Harris's work is difficult, they may be suffering from the unease of being on the frontier, and then a guide, albeit one who lays no claim to infallibility, can sometimes be helpful.

The first thing to note, as with all Harris's fiction, is that it straddles the frontier between prose and poetry. Bruce King has written:

> If Wilson Harris has any direct forebear it is T.S. Eliot with his meditations on time and tradition, and his fragmentation of narrative into a mosaic of dissociated images and symbols expressive of the chaos of modern culture and of the individual

mind attempting to piece together an encompassing vision out of personal disorder."[2]

In many ways, we should read Harris's fiction as we read "The Waste Land", attentive to its sonorities and rhythms, sensitive to its associations and the harmonics of its imagery, aware of its subcurrents of myth, patient in allowing the implications of the words and their combinations to unfold in the mind. Like fragrances on the palate, they come together in the firing of synaptic trees of intellectual meaning.

Harris's writing is consistent with the modernist project of seeing beneath and beyond the apparent surface realities and the constraints of cultural convention. The density of his prose opens out continually to numinous and memorable images, but also to vistas of insight and wisdom, reaching far beyond the limited perspectives of the time the book was written, just as Eliot's words echo far outside the mid-twentieth century. And Harris shares with Eliot deep roots in the landscape and poetics of both Europe and the Americas. It was Eliot, it will be recalled, who headed the firm which published Harris's first novel in 1960, and all his subsequent novels.

The Eye of the Scarecrow begins programmatically, in the framing device of a diary tracking of the novel's gestation, with an evocation of another type of frontier. The diary/journal entry, written in London in 1963, describes a sunset in Edinburgh. It envisions a point where day and night meet at the junction of earth, sea and sky, in which the tree outlined against the sunset shares the nature of the vegetable and animal realms, while the light behind it is a mixture of ice and fire, as at the start of the Norse creation myth. The author describes the meeting in terms of the spiritual world of consciousness and the material world upon which it depends becoming aware of each other. The entry is dated 25–26 December, possibly the actual date of composition of the novel, but by synchronicity also the solstice moment chosen for the celebration of the birth of a new spiritual principle. There is also a reflection here of the events in the writer's personal life which saw him establishing himself, like many West Indian compatriots, on the frontier shores of the metropolis, which often treated them as second-class and marginal. The landscapes of Guyana, the focus of the novels from *Palace of the Peacock* to *Heartland*, are now brought into contact with London and Edinburgh – home city of his wife and muse (and dedicatee of all the novels) Margaret – a sign both of the novels to come and of the way in which space is to be related to universality.

The coupling of two events in the year 1948 begins the second part of Book One. The strike in what was then British Guiana, a moment of great political significance for the country, but one whose expectations were not fulfilled, is set alongside a profoundly personal visionary moment. The narrator suddenly sees his friend L——'s face like the shattered, cracked surface of clay in a drought. This unexpected moment of seeing an apparent mask of material which allows both insight and reflection also involves a frontier: it will lead through a fascinating meditation to conclusions about the mysteries of difference and identity which recall and interrogate Donne's assertion that "No Man is an Iland, intire of it selfe". The scarecrow that emerges from the crumbling mask of a face has a dual character, both being terrifying because uncanny and smiling a welcome. There is also dual movement over the frontier of the consciousness, a penetration through the apparently hollow mask and unseeing eye to what lies beneath, and the multiplicity of the unconscious emerging to meet it. Harris was to return to this image again, most notably in *The Mask of the Beggar* (2003). The scarecrow imagery, and the images of crumbling and mask proliferate within other characters and descriptions, which all now take on this same valorization. There are, for example, the dying governor who rides past the narrator's house, the procession of strikers, the hearse-drivers, or the tenants of Waterloo Street. Later there will be Scarecrow himself, whose confession, *The Eye of the Scarecrow*, will be signed by Idiot Nameless on the level of the outer time-frame of 1964.

Thus the eye of the scarecrow may be, among other things, the lens through which consciousness may begin to perceive what it is afraid to see: the shadow side of its own personality, the personal unconscious, but far beyond that – what Harris has termed the universal unconscious – the world of the dead, the spirit of place, a realm of timelessness. For the narrator to penetrate that world will require such disorientation that he will be in danger of losing the attributes of consciousness and becoming both idiot and nameless, the *tumbe Tor* who alone can succeed in the Grail quest.[3]

So why is this personal and interior process coupled with the political events resulting from the historical and economic situation in British Guiana? It is one of the extraordinary features of Harris's fiction that he is able to relate the one to the other in ways that illuminate both and that have brought him recognition both as a postcolonial theorist and a groundbreaking literary practitioner. The result offers a fuller understanding of the limits of political potential in human nature, and the effect on human nature of political and economic injustice. In addition, through the interpenetration Harris describes, the restrictive bias of any one position of consciousness is gradually revealed to the reader.

The first book is preceded by two epigraphs. One is from the poem "The Broken Tower" by Hart Crane, a modernist poem which describes how the sound of bells before dawn allows access to a "visionary company of love" through which an immaterial tower can be built corresponding with the world. On the surface, the second epigraph, from Ecclesiastes, means that no one can prevent themselves from dying, but it can also be taken to mean that inspiration and vision cannot be commanded, but come and go irrespective of human will.

Bearing the two epigraphs in mind, we may approach the

first book as a series of recollections viewed and remade, like Crane's tower, through an interaction between memory, interpretation and inspiration, or what the narrator calls "the frail visionary organization of memory" (p. 34; page references to this edition). These memories, and the language used to describe them, echo through the rest of the novel. They all relate to Georgetown, but are not arranged chronologically. Apart from 1948, the year of the strike when the narrator sees the vision of the scarecrow in L——'s face – and the narrator must be twenty-seven – they are incidents from his childhood: looking at the Atlantic foreshore aged eight, seeing the "poor man's hearse" with its riders; watching a balloon with his nurse; having an operation (to remove the tonsils) in 1932; looking at the canal and trees outside his grandfather's house and imagining a hanging slave there; pushing L—— into the canal; seeing the governor riding past and associating it with the picture of the Battle of Waterloo, both in 1929; a visit to his grandfather's tenants in Waterloo Street; his convalescence after the operation and resuming eating; and the making of mud figures with L——.

It is worth having a closer look at some of the techniques Harris employs here. Familiarity with them may give the uncertain reader more confidence elsewhere. The section recalling the narrator's visit to his grandfather's tenants (pp. 45 – 49) may be taken as an illustration. Harris uses an underlying framework of narrative linked to images that, in turn, relate to further episodes and descriptions. The narrative involves the narrator and his grandfather walking between two rows of single-storey houses. The inhabitants of these houses are standing at their open doorways. Only one family is mentioned by name: the Anthrops, who are the only ones able to pay rent in a time of economic depression. The image of the lines of houses and the tree at the end is conjured up with suggestive realism, but once established, this vivid image is mined and modulated to create numerous levels of association and significance.

Firstly the narrative event is associated with the image that precedes it, an ellipsis in its turn of the dying governor and his orderly riding along an avenue in Georgetown with the ranks of soldiers in the painting of the Battle of Waterloo. Each element here contains its reverse: the governor, representing conquest, is dying, and the soldiers wounded and dying for him become the urge towards protest and independence. Thus the narrator and his grandfather in Waterloo Street take on the role of the orderly and governor and the tenants the role of the people. They are represented by Anthrop – an allusion to Anthropos, both Everyman and the archetypal and alchemical "Great Man", the collective Self of humanity. Their rent is thus paid somehow to the divine, represented as owner and demiurge (grandfather), and creative consciousness (narrator).

Beyond the property occupied by Anthrop lie an untidy tamarind tree and a range of outbuildings so dilapidated they have been condemned as eyesores by the authorities. And yet this unpromising and unpicturesque area of decay is described in terms of extraordinary and unexpected potential, without any need for demolition:

> The occasional dry sweeping fall of leaf and shell caught the outhouses which were crumbling themselves ripe and fast; a bill ruling the latter unfit was soon to be presented to the Legislative Assembly by the Member representing the Municipality. For who would deny that the time had come for every eyesore to be abolished? What profit remained in upholding an art of decay, a canvas of fertile humour, ugly faith, inane, impolitic, thick-skinned, primitive manifesto? Why preserve each brutal wall, judicious hinge, unscientific doorway scored all over by the knife of weather to gape as well as laugh at every patched fruit of initiation into the soil? And yet (wretched economics of nature) here was enthroned the golden centre of inspiration, the most subjective scarecrow earth of all like the religious currency of wood motivated equally by rooted instinct as by growing callouses upon a body of dense spirit leading to an immaterial element of indifference as the quicksilver rain is indifferent to the brightness of the sun.(p. 47)

16

Harris's transformation is achieved by allowing the descriptive epithets to slide over into other things they adhere to, and to associate with their opposites. The buildings are in an open net of shadow – open because it is merely shadow, but thus the opposite of net. The net is drawn by the brushwork of leaves, an image from painting, but the brush is then immediately associated with a sweeping fall of leaf. Now the image applies to a brush with which the area might be swept. The outbuildings are crumbling *ripe* and fast (my emphasis), so are now associated with fruit from a tree.

The uselessness of preserving the buildings revitalizes the art imagery in the words "art" and "canvas", but extends it into "manifesto". Being ways of communicating allows them to use humour and personifies the buildings themselves with a collection of negative attributes: ugly, inane, impolitic, thick-skinned, brutal and unscientific, which become the unthinking condemnation contained in "gape" and "laugh". Scattered within them, light among shadow, are words expressing a more positive outcome: "fertile", "faith" and "judicious", before the image of fruit returns (with "patched" to recall both the shadow and repaired buildings) in the open earth by the tree, which becomes an area of initiation, of seeding. The doorway "scored all over by the knife of weather (p 47)" conjures a powerful vision of grey, grainy, weathered wood, which now takes on, as it were, the whole weight of the outbuildings, before the true kernel of the whole passage emerges as the "golden centre of inspiration". Here the "scarecrow earth", now elided with the cracked wood to recall L——'s face, is connected to the tree itself with its roots and calluses as the material being refreshed and nourished by sunlight and rain. The material is now "dense spirit" but in communion (a "religious currency") with the immaterial above it, using rain as a catalyst. This principle of organic growth from apparently dead material is the basis of fundamental alchemical processes, which required the spirit Mercurius as a trickster to help the transformation to fruition. So it is no wonder that the rain, sparkling liquid in the sun, is described as quicksilver (or mercury). To complete the paragraph, the alchemical image is extended by describing the creation of immateriality as an experiment, arising from the melting-pot of the material, now broadened in scope through the phrase "long-suffering geography of history" into a political dimension of space and time, and reminding the reader that all that has gone before is an image which needs to be applied to concrete circumstances.

While the narrator is walking he experiences a feeling of dizziness or unconsciousness, in which he does not notice that he and his grandfather have turned round and are coming back – this is not described explicitly but by analogy to what has happened to the narrator on a trip up the river – so that to him there seems to have been a strange process of reversal in which everything becomes its opposite. Part of this process involves the reversal of the living and the dead, which is another dimension of the meeting between consciousness and the material. The twins at their mother's breast in Anthrop's house become associated with the hearse-riders – the hearses containing either corpses or nothing – a sight which has previously disturbed the narrator, and thus also are associated with the dying governor and the dying victors (protesters) of Waterloo.

This sense of access to a world of opposites that are twinned, and to the twinning of the world with its opposites, is the eye of the scarecrow itself. The narrator experiences it here as a loss of orientation, a sense of the "stigmata of the void (p. 48)". The void for Harris is not mere negativity or nihilism, but a zero which, like Shakespeare's "wooden O", becomes the whole globe, an opening through time and fruitful space generated by language, in which being mixes and breeds with non-being and anything can be created by nothing. Its effect is one of stigmata, because it is the equivalent of the cross which Christians believe can bridge the inherent contradictions of human existence, the paradoxical tensions between spiritual awareness and the exigencies of the material.

Harris speaks about this void in essays contemporary with the novel, calling it "the enigmatic *void* of a new profound language to melt the abortive gesticulation of the world".[4] Thus Harris's density of image is not a mannerism, but, as I have suggested above, the only way of achieving the goal he has set himself, a "concept of language [...] which continuously transforms inner and outer formal categories of experience" leading to "a continuous inward revisionary and momentous logic of potent explosive images evoked in the mind".[5] Harris asserts:

> The medium of language, the poet's word (and this is essentially every man's true expression), is much more than a question of emotional and intellectual usage or documentary coinage. In fact to hint at *medium* is to embrace a vision of patterns and capacities beneath and beyond every game of one-sided meaning.[6]

If we, as readers, allow Harris's prose to work on us in this poetic way, the associations throughout the book will begin to become clearer. It will be seen that the narrator (the artist investigating the immaterial) and L—— (the scientist and engineer of the material) are two aspects of a single personality whose relationship is yet to be established. The figures of old and young (grandfather and grandson), of the hearse-riders and the animals they control, and of the disappearing or hidden mother-figure all reverberate through the novel at various removes from the original statement of the theme. At the same time all the other dimensions I have indicated are interwoven with these basic elements.

Two further archetypal "explosive images" present in the first book should also be brought into sharper focus. One is the incident which occurs in 1929 by one of Georgetown's canals, when the narrator, inquisitive to know how deep the canal is, pushes his friend L—— in. The repentant narrator escapes punishment because he is not blamed by L——, a connivance of loyalty and false memory which leaves them in a symbiotic relationship of shared responsibility and gratitude, a theme which Harris returns to later in the novel, and indeed in many subsequent novels. The incident is introduced by a description of the trees alongside the canal shepherding the moving water, which mutates into the image of the reflections (boys and trees) as a flock being shepherded. This description echoes that at the start of the book, when the flock is both the blank pages waiting to be written and the clouds shepherded by the sun. It will become more significant in Book Three when the collision with a grazing animal occurs at Raven's Head, and the driver (who is simultaneously two people) receives food and shelter from a shepherd and his grandson. This is another example of a technique of mystic association which sets up a chain of subliminal connections, advancing on a broad front like a wave, which resonate in the unconscious but with familiarity begin to achieve enigmatic conscious form.

A more readily graspable leitmotiv is the quote from St John's Gospel (14,2): "In my Father's house are many mansions", Jesus's words at the Last Supper. This indication of a plurality of redemption recalls the windows of the Palace of the Peacock and is a cautionary note to warn against any single interpretation of the novel, or any other path to consciousness.

Book Two – Genesis – opens with a biblical epigraph describing the emergence of Man from the material, which requires the breath of the spirit. The narrator has criticized L——'s mud figures, lifeless material unconvincingly made, which now appear different because of the spirit with which they are seen. At the same time this revelation makes the narrator aware of the cruelty he has inflicted on L—— by not seeing the causes of what he is. The same sharing of responsibility and guilt (started in the canal incident) is now worked into further variations on generations (old and young) and twinships, for example of poor Anthrop in Waterloo Street and rich Anthrop the civil engineer. The identity of the body becomes something indistinct and fluid, what Sara Upstone refers to as the "postcolonial chora".[7]

The mirroring of the narrator's mother glimpsed in a mirror behind a closing door and the moment of seeing Anthrop's wife hidden behind him leads into a whirling meditation on time and space from the Georgetown of childhood memories, the 1948 strike, or even the future of 2048. Now, having arrived at the midpoint of the novel, and having established an interior landscape which confirms paradox and contradiction as given – where all things relate to their opposites, as youth and age complement each other like suffering and oppression, and where the living are the dead and vice versa – the narration shifts its setting to the Guyanese interior, but not in a sense of overt realism, except in as much as images depend on objective correlatives. In that sense the descriptions recall details of the landscape around Bartica. The narrator speaks here of a project, shared between himself and L——, of rediscovering mythical gold in the rainforest at the site of a mining town called Raven's Head.

The myth of gold in the interior is at least as old as the European discovery of Guiana; Raleigh staked his life on the legend of El Dorado. In reading Harris, we must be aware that gold in an alchemical sense is a spiritual mystery linked to the material, so in the novel it is inextricable from the spirit of place, which in turn is inseparable from the people whose life and cosmology was bound up with this land. Thus Raven's Head is also another name for the native woman, Hebra, treated by the narrator and L—— as a prostitute, in their own slightly different ways, as they try to penetrate her/the place's mystery. For L—— it is an engineering problem which needs solving – of finding the site and transporting dredging equipment; for the narrator it is a continuing dismantling of the motivations and execution of such plans in order to make them conscious in the wider dimensions he has been establishing.

We suddenly find ourselves, with the narrator and L——, on a suspension bridge, apparently built by the narrator's stepfather. This is on the one hand a material bridge, admired by L—— for its engineering precision, crossing an arm of the river near Sorrow Hill. From this perspective it can be treated geographically, in exterior space, as Sorrow Hill (or Sarah Hill) is a graveyard on a ridge near the town of Bartica, portal to the rainforest interior where the Cuyuni and Mazaruni rivers join the Essequibo. On the other hand it is in suspension from the material world, a rainbow bridge, associated through imagery with Hebra herself, from where the "dazzling sleeper of spirit (p. 63)" can be observed awaking to new life. A further strand of the imagery, however, is that of hanging (suspension, execution, trapdoor), echoing similar chords of imagery in Books One and Three and stressing the perilous nature of what the Grail search means. (It may be recalled that in John Boorman's film *Excalibur* the Grail quest involved the hanging of the hero by the enchantress Morgana.) It is only at the moment of suspension between life and death that the seeker learns the secret of the Grail (that the land and the king are one) and so ushers in the redemption of the waste land. He becomes nothing (Idiot Nameless) in accepting the guilt of the oppressor and the pain of the oppressed. When a noose closes on nothing it disappears, allowing an opening to unpredictable freedom. The bridge will also be the construction of the novel itself (from notes and snapshots of memory) when the author is attempting an expedition into the unconscious, and so gives a dreaming postal address of Night's Bridge (or Knightsbridge, London, or the bridge of the Grail Knight).

This expedition is the matter of Book Three, entitled Raven's Head. This time the epigraphs stress the material and the spiritual, old and new, and the eye, which we suggested earlier is the eye of the scarecrow itself, the lens of Raven's Head through which consciousness and the unconscious begin to see each other. There are four approaches, or gates, to Raven's Head. The four-gated city is an archetypal representation of the alchemical *lapis*, the completed Self where the opposites are reconciled, represented by the Tibetan mandala or the patterns of Amerindian weaving. The approach from the north, from Georgetown, is the approach from colonizing consciousness. But from this side the blinkered horse shies at the phantom sound of a discontinued colonial gun, paralysing the will to go forward. Sorrow Hill, the eastern gate, is the gate of death itself, while the western gate, the suspension bridge, does not allow access or engagement with the mystery. Thus it is the southern gate, Hebra's gate, which must be used, coming through the experience gained in the heartland of the previous novels.

The best way to approach Book Three is by analogy with a dream, which uses the guise of elements from the material world to investigate the depths of the psyche, and, following Jung, not only of the personal unconscious but of a collective and universal substrate or pattern which is not usually accessible to consciousness. At first reading it may seem that the "crash" experienced (in car or plane) by the driver (or drivers) represents accurately the feelings of a reader used to smooth narrative progress. From now on a different narrative pattern, more akin to dreaming, prevails. The crash represents another frontier, or barrier, at one point described as "paper-thin" to stress its intimate bond with the fiction itself, but which does not involve a goal, a static place, but a further ongoing process. Hena Maes-Jelinek points out that: "*The Eye of the Scarecrow* reaches no definite conclusion"; it is a "continuous progress through the moving contrasts of existence".[8]

What might this crash be? In the forward technological drive powered by a newly emerging dual nature (manifest in the altered perception of the relationship between the narrator and L——), consciousness has collided with something resistant, part active (as a tiger), part passive (as a cow), both inanimate and organic. He (the narrative voice, now shifting between first and third person) has reached a centre where he is confronted by a mythological female minotaur which represents the spirit of place – and is thus associated with the Amerindians' spiritualization of the land – and the muse of his inspiration, soul-image and material lure. In the confrontation he has also reached the centre of his own being, having crossed and recrossed a mysterious canal, amid images of childhood, to revisit key moments of his life, but in aligning that centre or soul with his own desires, his own conceptions (or misconceptions) of beauty and ugliness, he has fixed his desire to a material economy. Thus the salesman of shoes and the beggar on Water Street reverse the laws of supply and demand; the danger of the muse as material lure is echoed in her danger as spiritual obsession. The sense of a closed mind and an imprisoning verdict is conveyed by the ambiguity of the word "conviction". It is only through an understanding of the relationship between lust and love that he can simultaneously destroy the power of this muse (an act of murder) while accepting the humility and capacity of the vision she brings (converting it into an *art* of murder).

If the muse is overcome in this way, it is possible to advance to a further frontier beyond a sense of guilt or an endless "procession of the ages" in which nothing is learnt from experience. The author writes at this point:

> For if indeed his jealous claim to the art of murder remained unflinching and still sensitive to truth, might he not have succeeded beyond his wildest dreams in supporting and re-creating the enigma of life – the twins of breath and breathlessness, animus and anima? Future instinct of the borderline. To be or not to be. (p.100)

The secret of the twinship between Hamlet the father and Hamlet the son, and the consequences of unreflecting desire on Gertrude or Ophelia (as mother/muse) or on the murderer/victim, lies in understanding the relationship between being and non-being, which is to understand how art interacts with the ground of experience revealed as marked, scored and grained, like weathered wood.

In this context it is perhaps interesting to note that Hebra, the name of the muse / prostitute (and of the legendary town itself) means in Spanish the grain in wood, or a seam of coal or ore. It will be seen that this is an image, associated with organic growth and mineral deposit, for patterns which exist in the material world yet move beyond it. Hollowed out, it could represent a container through which liquid or sound might flow, familiar from Harris's writings as the Amerindian bone flute, through which conquest and destruction gave access to spiritual values. What appears silent (or silenced) becomes a well from which living waters may flow (the well of silence).

Value comes through the use of language, so when the prison-like walls closing in are shown to become insubstantial, the "Manifesto of the Unborn State of Exile" sums up what we have already *sensed* throughout the novel: the way language reveals the relationship between the inner and outer eye – to transcend itself through its own grain (as wood or seed or the basis of an economy) so that this "granular" language can interact with the material rather than just acting as a "preservative fluid" to record reality. And language, of course, is not merely a dialogue within the fictional text but also exists on a further frontier between the text and the reader as "silent words on their speaking page" (p. 107) through the intervention (on both sides) of Imagination (which at this point in the text is capitalized as a transcendent faculty).

Through Imagination (working with and on unreliable memory by correspondence and intuition) it has become possible to see how everything is at least double in a pattern of quantum indeterminacy that allows for concrete, material identity while denying its apparent substance, thus allowing ego consciousness access to the unconscious. Paget Henry, in writing about Harris, calls this "an imagination that has been schooled in the quantum literacy of consciousness".[9] So Raven's Head, the alternative name of Hebra, with its forbidding gates, depends on the presence of death, but is also the *nigredo* which ushers in the alchemical transformation to the *cauda pavonis*,

25

the peacock's tail, leading to the *lapis*, the true gold or alchemist's stone of timeless life. The raven, divine bird of Norse mythology, is also the crow, a bird of fearful death. To look into its scarecrow eye is to confront an awe-ful presence, and to overcome it.

Finally, in the coda to the novel, themes are recalled in the "Black Rooms" of the first two books, before, at the junction of the two temporal levels of the narration, the final mystery of identity is restated: that what at first appears to be a fixed frame of time and space becomes a timeless quantum amalgam of the two and the one, the two to prevent the rigid bias of any single vision by insisting on its opposite, in order to rehabilitate "the lost One, the unrealized One, the inarticulate One", before the final note of prayer fades into the replenished well of silence.

ENDNOTES

1. T.S. Eliot, *On Poetry and Poets* (London: Faber and Faber, 1957), p. 115.
2. Quoted in Anita Patterson, *Race, American Literature and Transnational Modernisms* (Cambridge: CUP, 2008), p. 130.
3. The 'simple fool' is the proverbial designation in medieval German applied to Parzival, the Grail Knight in Wolfram von Eschenbach's 13th Century romance, who, having been brought up in ignorance of the ways of the world, can approach it with a new consciousness.
4. Wilson Harris, "Books – a Long View", in *Tradition, the Writer and Society* (London: New Beacon Books, 1967), p. 23.
5. Wilson Harris, "Tradition and the West Indian Novel", ibid., p. 32.
6. Wilson Harris, "Books – a Long View", ibid., p. 21.
7. Plato uses the term chora to mean receptacle, or "situation for all things that come into being". As such it has been widely discussed by feminist and postcolonial theorists in

relation to the body. Upstone writes: "In the chora, the chaos that the colonial world would cast as dangerous in its attempts to produce easily categorized and controllable bodies is exactly what is utilised to engender creation. Fluid and indissolubly linked to what surrounds it [...], the displacement of the body in the spirit of the chora so that it mingles with other bodies and objects does not produce psychosis, as psychoanalysts suggest. Rather, [...] what emerges is a positive event." Sara Upstone, *Spatial Politics in the Postcolonial Novel* (Farnham: Ashgate, 2009), p. 164.

8. Hena Maes-Jelinek, *The Labyrinth of Universality* (Amsterdam & New York: Rodopi, 2006), p. 167.

9. Paget Henry, *Caliban's Reason* (New York: Routledge, 2000), p. 108.

BOOK ONE

THE VISIONARY COMPANY

And so it was I entered the broken world
To trace the visionary company of love, its voice
An instant in the wind...

HART CRANE

There is no man that hath power over the spirit
to retain the spirit.

ECCLESIASTES viii, 8

1

25th–26th December 1963   This year in the autumn I visited the ancient city of Edinburgh, travelled across the rim of the windswept Pentlands and descended to the steel-grey Firth of Forth...

One pause of sunset, in particular, I recall now, like a station of feathered branches, half-tree, half-bird, lingering a long while in the sky before a train of frozen fire part-extinguished, part-melted itself into the ground. In the fulfilled poise of this moment, like a barrier of absorption between day and night, the reluctant smoke of sky and carriage of earth were drawn into singular consciousness of each other...

Now as I make this – the first entry in this Journal – the winter sky of London travels through the window and falls upon the page before me like the blank fleece of a wayward flock, wayward yet still shepherded by the overcast sun, all shorn to spread in such an absent moment an intimate landscape and illumination.

The entries of an experience related to *1948* will be written far outside of that year. The fact is I am only now about to embark on making these. Nevertheless – late as it seems – I am hoping it may prove the first reasonable attempt (my Journals in the past were subject to the close tyranny and prejudice of circumstance) at an open dialogue within which a free construction of events will emerge in the medium of phenomenal associations all expanding into a mental distinction and life of their own.

The question arises – who or what indeed is this medium of capacity, this rift uncovering a stranger animation one senses within the cycle of time and the hub of another state of apparent unawareness?...

2

1948
WATER STREET

28th December 1963   Nineteen forty-eight, the year of the Guiana Strike, uncertain forerunner of private upheaval and public change in the decades which followed, may now well be symbolically described as another year of local climax for some, universal anticlimax for others. I remember I met L——— early in the year before anything serious had actually happened anywhere as far as I knew. His face wore a normal expression. Still I glanced away abruptly as if involuntarily conscious of something I did not wish to see, then turned back and confronted him again feeling suddenly stricken with foreboding and astonishment. In that instant of my turning away and back again every feature of his appeared shattered, like the smooth but cracked surface of a depression, after a naked spell of drought... The incredible image of a scarecrow vanished, as if in passing it had never existed and L———'s face was smiling at some current joke he was telling, his eyes moist as the reflection of rain. He was unaware of anything abnormal in the motionless heat of the day. The silent thunderclap I had heard so loud in my imagination (and which he had in some lightning way invoked) had been an instantaneous explosion, which left not an echo of trespass or crisis upon him though a curious void of conventional everyday feeling began from that moment to take the shape of a moving cloud in my mind.

12th–15th February 1964   Much as I would like to recall – like a ghost returning to the past – the identical map of place which

32

was shattered in a moment I cannot. I cannot remember the colour of the paint on the walls of L——'s room; and only with a great effort am I able to establish that there were others present, a couple of draughtsmen perhaps, in the room which served as L——'s engineering office.

This effort of memory still cannot restore more than an assumption of an essential fabric of person and thing; which hallucinatory furniture appears swept clean – at this distant remove in time and place – of flesh or grit like smooth slabs, neither paper nor stone, in a skeletal grain of bleached wood.

The fact is I find myself conferring the curious baptism of living imagination upon helpless relics, relics which thereby lose a smothering or smothered constitution and character. For if I were to attempt to confine or draw an exact relationship or absolute portrait of what everything was before the stroke fell and created a void in conventional memory, I would have succumbed to the dead tide of self-indulgent realism. On the other hand, to travel with the flood of animated wreckage that followed after, is a different matter, a trusting matter in which I am involved – a confession that nothing immaterial and actual and eternal may have changed in the outlines of the past; and therefore since the nucleus of phenomenal catastrophe one envisages at any particular moment is just as likely as anything else to be an illusion, it is useless to believe one was, or is, ever possessed by articles of spirit without faith.

I am beginning to see now at last, more clearly than ever, why I must never cease to question every vehicle of self-sufficient recollection... The senses of apprehension which endure today within me, to approach a distant place and time, have truly dwindled into correspondences and intuitions. And these are declining still further even now into the purest, frailest instinct of an incalculable faith in a freedom of being.

L——'s room stood at the top of two storeys whose windows glanced in the sunlight across Water Street towards the burning estuary of the Demerara river where the crest of a wave occasionally flickered as if it sought a pencil of relief (or was it extinction?) beneath the shadow of pavement on the sea wall withstanding the Atlantic…

It is this frail visionary organization of memory – one thing against another, and everything apparently laying siege to nothing (while nothing seems to extend into the immaterial capacity and absorption of everything) – which highlights the transient figures of the insensible past into ideal erections against chaos, standing within a measureless ground plan of spiritual recognitions, intimacies and identities…

As a child of eight, nineteen years before the great Strike, I climbed the mound – at the northern extremity of Water Street – towards the wall overlooking the river's mouth in the Atlantic. That was long before the Municipal Authority had thought of erecting a bath-hut and converting the desolate foreshore into an open swimming pool. No one was around (or if there was I have now forgotten) but I still remember clearly the spirit which moved in that place; and the dislocated image which returns seems strangely to address me within the beckoning associations not only of 1948 but of 1964 when this late entry in time is being made. The air over the foreshore was filled with a tumultuous cloud of palm flies, flying wires of insects with gauze-like wings which seemed, in their cloud-like angelic transparency, like the subtlest dispersal in nature of a nameless fear of demons: the flying wisp of a bandage torn from the blank compulsive heart of sickness and death, the crippled self-deception of beggars – stationed in the shadow of the commercial houses of Water Street as in a depression in a mental landscape (that worldwide depression of the 1920s and 30s) – protesting with the greatest unconscious eloquence, born of a kind of degrading hollow silence, to be rarefied and uplifted from being mere chains upon themselves and rooted stumps and imprisoned castaways.

17th–29th February 1964   And it is along Water Street, a mere trickle of legend in 1948, that a funeral procession returns to my mind's eye like the beginnings of a swollen flood in the world of 1964. The anonymous light but tragic spring of the dead moves secretly and steadfastly across every continent in every falling raindrop. Light as a feather, yet capable of descending like a stone.

I see now through the conscious mask of winter how slowly it seemed then sixteen years ago in the impatient heat of the pitiless struggle, that the unconscious spring of death had come; the longed-for, renascent yet dreadful arrival of incipient maturity: the faces of those who shot up, prematurely, with a conviction of self-righteous organization, and died before they knew it in the battle of the year, strike and lock-out... The signal procession of cars, horse-drawn vehicles, ancient buses, bicycles, men, women, children came half-limping, half-rolling, along the flat coastal road, canvassing the country for the greatest possible witness of support – across the imperceptible relief of the Demerara/Mahaica watershed – descending though unaware of it (the ground looked so uniform) into an erasure of old plantation boundaries forming the Demerara township and capital – pressing into the line of the wall against the sea and advancing to meet the river's estuary... There it turned into Water Street.

One nightmare account accused the native officers of the police of commanding (out of misjudgment ripening into bestiality and fear) their loyal ranks to open fire too quickly – another said cryptically that those who worked to sow the dragon's teeth deserved whatever they got. And it was here – at the crossroads of history (as the placards borne aloft by the revolutionaries in the procession declared) – that the confusing limits of tragedy became apparent in the shattering question of unity: did the stress of comradeship lie in all visualizing and uprooting a guilty motive from amongst themselves and – in exposing each other's mental crime – submitting to the forced

35

spring of movement (however false and untimely) of all?...
Such a questionable union involved the hideous and logical
denigration of every person, high and low, in the horror of a
progressive realism which was far more dangerous, because it
seemed politic and necessary however aimless and subversive,
than the most fertile incestuous fantasy. It was the devil's abyss
blocking the way, I dreamt (as if every hopeful intuition I
possessed was now all at once overturned in the midst of
unexpected perils), the irony and nihilism of spirit I suddenly
saw which bore such a close, almost virtuous, resemblance to
the unprejudiced reality of freedom I was seeking to entertain;
and one found oneself peering, as a consequence, into the heart
of the universal carnival for the grimmest redeeming clue of an
open memory, the germ of associating sovereign truth and
humility...

There was the sudden awakening clatter of horses' hooves
close at hand magnetized into acute consciousness by the
mildewed repellent odour of sliced leather or dung which
burnt my nostrils: and this harness of sensation was drawn in
the same instant into a wilder contorted outrider of shadow –
the common-or-garden vulture flapping its wings grotesquely;
it had arisen clumsily after being disturbed from picking at
shreds on the foreshore. It appeared at first as if it could not fail
to fall like an ungainly hoof and strike its own rebellious spark
on the ground but adjusted its flight and strode, phenomenal
poise, equal power, beyond L——'s gaping window into the
soaring distance of clouds burning in the sun.

The sharp sound of primary hooves and the torn smell of a
sick half-eaten body of leather – combined with the scarecrow
of shadow alighting for a flashing moment upon the funeral
procession – issued into the starkest bier of grave memory I
knew, when as a boy on my way to school I sometimes
encountered the "poor man's hearse" rolling towards me,
painted black as shining coal.

Rumour circulated the facts – rumour which had long lost

its human tongue and facts which existed in the deaf light of some curious unswerving heedless direction – that the nameless paupers of charity who occupied an obscure ward in the Public Hospital were vagrants of the soul and therefore long before each one expired he (or she) was in process of being borne to his (or her) end within an unconscious design, perpetuating the self-sufficient life of doom, the seal upon all eyes, on all the senses of the world, on every visual and palpable certainty that one existed in the corruption of flesh. And I knew no one *knew* for certain that anyone or anything lay in the interior of the blind hearse as it rolled past, which, unlike every prepossessing vehicle of the dead, lacked sides of glass through which the onlooker could spy the shape of a coffin under its growth of flowers. If the two were to confront one another, as sometimes inadvertently happened, the poor man's singular hoax face to face with a number of conventional mourning carriages, the mêlée which ensued cast an engulfing shadow on the blatant capsule of day. No wonder the ghostly idiot stranger and spectator in one's own breast – plunged into awareness of how deprived one was of root and reality – started prompting one to wonder indeed whether the blossoming casket in clear view carried rags of nothing within, or the wheat of something without, resembling a shattered loaf for this or that nonexistent stomach.

And as the black solitary hearse grew nearer I was stricken by the devouring faces of the two men, the hearse-riders, sitting high in front, laughing and joking, totally oblivious to my frenzied countenance (as if I were the meagre necessary grain of spirit they had stored out of sight and blissfully forgotten in their own miserly contrivance of a tomb); oblivious, too, of the horses' reins as if these dangled from another's – my own? – life-giving hands. They might have been incapable of truly hearing or speaking or both, while unfeeling and unseeing in the bargain, and the mirth which issued from their lips is still a riddle which taxes all, day in, day out.

That I may still recall them to the consciousness of the living for the merrymaking bread of sustenance, and they may continue forever to bear my vestigial parts in their dense spirit of self-mockery of death – is a sufficient, indeed alarming, witness of a mutual and living god, the uncommitted nurses of dialogue between agents and persons unknown and things and places unapprehended.

As fearfully and inevitably as the explosive train of memory rolls along (mingling economic and political, metaphysical and dialectical physicians like an ancestral gathering of nurses to help one stomach the banquet of the dead), there follows in its wake the consciousness of a dream: I had my finger upon a trigger – departed lives fired again to ricochet like bullets within the corridors of the mind. *In my Father's house are many mansions.* I dreamt I was standing alone in a large room and the question arose – where did the dying procession of strikers vanish? Were they swallowed in the abyss of Water Street or did they find consolation in some funereal cellar corresponding to the burning of all material ambition? I found myself confronted by a mystery, the mystery involved in a decision to seek those, whom the rage for an ideal may have consumed, down one fiery way or along another which would permit me to retrace my own steps in time.

The room in which I stood was part of a building of two storeys. It may have been my grandfather's lodge in East Street, the meeting place of a small religious group; on the other hand it looked equally like L——'s engineering office in Water Street... I had left my step-grandmother downstairs in the company of other women, cousins and servants of this nebulous establishment. I had been looking out of a window in their company when there rose before me, high in the sky, a purplish balloon, half-carriage, half-bird, floating above the housetops. I suspected who the inmates were – officials and directors of church and state, by whom I was employed to serve in an obscure alchemical capacity, and since I was on sick leave I did not wish to be seen up and about by them. Even as I looked the balloon came down right next door. I turned away from the window and hurriedly began to ascend the stairs, followed by a solicitous attendant, the shadow of the woman who had nursed me in the earliest years I could remember. Her name was Cromwell or Crumbwell or the crumb (of reality) – WHICH–MAKES–WELL. I was grateful for her attention and for the opportunity to explain to her why I had left the company in such haste; and I persuaded her to watch for the arrival of my hypothetical employers... On her reluctant departure I was left alone to explore the large upper room in which I was now aware – as if for the first time – of a number of royally made beds, unwrinkled sheets and blankets. These seemed to me, however, merely the dutiful ward of ruling substitutes in which my heart was now truly sick. I discovered a door in the wall I had never seen before opening into a secret apartment and I stopped dead on the threshold. It seemed an exotic and self-effacing, even subversive retreat to find and yet curiously logical and right in its context, when one bore in mind the paradoxical unity of this commanding house devoted to the religious observance of an absent proprietor and utilitarian conscience. As I stared into it I was overwhelmed for it was – beyond a shadow of doubt – the revolutionary goal I pursued, another bedchamber but this time (unlike the expansive day-light one in which I still stood) devoid of every film or integument of a window. Nevertheless however cloistered it first appeared – it was filled with a rust-coloured light like ammunition fired from distant stars, naked metallic rose, neither iron nor bronze nor gold: the sleep of an immaterial unsupported element: the armour of the poor, and I knew then how dread and necessary it was to dream to enter the striking innermost chemistry of love, transcending every proud cham-ber in the inexorable balloon of time.

3

1929-32
EAST STREET AND WATERLOO

1st March–7th May   At the age of eleven – in the year 1932— I spent a month in Public Hospital during which I underwent a serious operation. Chloroform. Sickly-sweet smell one never gets rid of, the half-smell of life and of death. The garden of disgust. Bewildering and nauseating fantasy akin to the strangest recollection of riding out of the womb. Finding oneself ushered into and out of a galloping skin. What consciousness of relief to discover one simulates dying in order to live, and pretends remembering when (or how) one was born in order to reassure oneself one lives and must die… For the thought of eternity – unless punctuated by such inflections of relief, hiatus or cessation – would be an unbearable inflation of terror and inhuman timelessness… I lay still under the chloroform – which had been administered by the dutiful hands of my nurse – and stared at corrugations on the slanting roof of a house, white, opaque, and yet inclined to give out such an intensity of suppressed radiant emotion one could almost *feel* an illusion of weight and of weightlessness.

I emerged with a constricting stamen of anxious blood in my throat and was borne away on a stretcher to be fed on liquids. Like a plant in a pot… The garden in front of my grandfather's house was full of voices and flowers at this time of the year, the month of March, the full-blooded hue and cry of tropical spring. A donkey was braying as it appeared to run before its pursuing cart, dogs were barking against the wheels following animal feet. Grasses and blooms, not only loud reds but silent yellows, the sweetpea, the sunflower, kept pace with me on

40

either side of the echoing flagged pathway as one ran from the front steps to the front gate which opened on to East Street. Then there was the abrupt signal of water dividing East Street into northern and southern banks or roadways, and along the striding parapets close to this fluid boundary moved stately pillars of trees. For this waterway was an artery and reserve once within the radius of an anchored plantation encompassing successive owners – French, Dutch, English, African and Indian stock, but now propelled by the stalwart trunks of legacies sharing both obsessions of shadow and circumference. I used to immure myself and stand at the window of the deepset house to glimpse the sliced surface of the canal. The water level sometimes stood fresh and high, shimmering with corrugations in the wind, the tracery of steel, veins of shadow, the enormous outline of frail fingers like elongated petals cast by the high, dark, green and swaying body of a spirit in the trees against the clouds. These would all sound and speak together when the rope of wind sharpened and blew, an extraordinary dense gallows of movement, the hanged trespasser within the sentence of place, the broadcast of an ancient execution and runaway design. It was an unparallelled vision of seed and fruit, the saddle of history and the captive of nature, the recollections of one who shared the severance and the unity of ancestral master and slave. When I spoke of the ghost I saw to my grandfather, half in judgment, half in jest, he burst into a great rage. It was the first time I had seen him so angry. I felt chastened and stricken for confessing to what he declared in my present imagining was no longer the brutal punishment inflicted upon one man by his time but gross self-indulgence followed by pride. Such idolatrous realism he would not tolerate even in an unhappy child. And from that moment my pagan scaffold, my visionary sport in nature, began crumbling secretly beyond the limits of the purity of obsession… And yet little though I knew it this was to prove a lifetime's poetry of science and a stubborn terrifying task. It was to prove the reliving of all my life again and again as if I were a ghost returning to the same place (which was always different), shoring up different ruins (which were always the same).

L—— was one of my first childhood friends, soon to be left an orphan by his mother's sudden death. He was then sent to an institution but he visited me from time to time and on each occasion I seemed to recall differently the memory of what occurred between us on the banks of the East Street canal… It was 1929, three years before my sudden operation that turned its uprooting light on everything like a decisive culminating blend of awareness serving to endorse and create (in a process whose art was one of the purest eradication) the youngest mental and oldest timeless scars…

L—— and I were standing half in the shade of one of the great trees which shepherded the canal along, intent on our own flock of reflections hanging in the water and I was filled with overwhelming curiosity. How could I measure the binding depth of the crowded stream? I instantly pushed L——— in before I realized what I was doing. He fell into the water with a choked outcry and I was filled only then – when it was too late – with remorse and alarm. I leaned over quickly, frightened at what I had done, and gripped his hand, noting, however, at the same time in the insensitive way one gratifies an instinctive curious appetite that the water seemed no higher than his chest against the side of the canal. I pulled and he scrambled to regain the land and I saw from his condition that if he had been double his slight build he might have sunken very deep into the bottom of the canal. As it was his feet were now long-booted and leaden with mud, his clothing foul, dripping and wrinkled into the alien folds of another skin. He was trembling with shock, so much so I was privi-leged to escape the direct sting of punishment. His memory played an evasive trick on him. When asked by my grandfa-ther to tell what had actually happened he declared he had suddenly slipped and fallen of his own accord. He did not dare to dream anyone (least of all myself) had in reality given him the slightest push.

In this unwitting way he had saved me from the wrath of justice and I had involuntarily and compulsively pushed him into becoming my own gauge of future extremity. This dawning conscience within me of the guilt of freedom was due to his insensibility and instrumentality: while the childish and child-like knowledge which prompted him to assume my enduring innocence was due to my concurrence in his early stumbling of faith in a universal external liability, the commission of error and weakness I found myself unwilling and unable to explain to him he did not entirely and solely possess... Was his privilege greater than mine because of my debt to his unwitting magnanimity or did mine exceed his since it was I who *knew* the instinctive scale and (unpardonable?) reflex of reality which elevated him in all dumb honesty and excuse above myself?... This was the suspended root of a question within a question I began dimly to transplant beyond the premises of immediate judgment on myself.

If indeed one were to conceive of each growing point in the judgment of experience – whether the ghost of any year such as 1932 back to the uncertain body of 1929, or the certain body of 1964 melting into the ghost of 1948 – as an intimate transplantation of the broken texture and fruit of time in oneself – pointing towards the ultimate uprooting of all pre-conception in the humility of consciousness – one is bound to marvel at the stubborn renascence and proliferation of the past returning out of every desired goal of nothingness, out of the pitiful seed of vanquished memory, in the midst of evacuation and detritus cast forth from a hollowness of spirit in the service of science or art, law or love. Is it that within the rubble of oneself still lies the key...?

An early childhood companion such as L——, who grows into my closest friend over the years and yet seems totally insensitive to my every mood of crisis so that sometimes it is on the tip of my tongue to accuse him of being deaf and dumb, lives to engineer, I feel, a certain living retrenchment, in those who are aware, of the dead rule of pride: grandfather's puritanical love of justice suffers as a dead consequence in my living time, his stern invariable injunction – to uproot each material god one is forever inclined to uphold – flags and wilts of itself within the poetic logic of the years and survives only by transplanting the ground of itself into a humbler agnostic reflection of the sovereign loss or gain of a property of place. *He would turn against me now if he knew*. For indeed I cannot tell what evil inspiration prompted me, all of a sudden, to reduce him into my daemon and agnostic. Was it the ghost of himself, posthumous irony? No, how could this be, when such an apparition would stun and appal him? I hear his voice from the grave repudiating everything, accusing me, once again, of fabricating a lie – self-indulgence followed by... not pride this time, surely, but the retrenchment of proper pride, the reduction of a proper and sound regard for him. How could I accept this licence to operate upon my own self-appointed guardian of conscience? How could I dream to engage in the subversion of his classic principle? His religious truth of abstention from notions of exaggerated innocence or guilt in regard to the time and place of others is in process of being converted by me into the strangest consistency – the worship of an insensible knife-edge of moving compassion upon all persons and things. And this places me in a peculiar position to exercise peculiar judgment upon him in the realm of his withdrawal into a privileged establishment of trust which may not, after all, be *his* but *my* conceit.

Equally (for one such as myself who confesses himself doomed to live and repair, in a battle with my own will, as it were, the crumbling senses of corruption the other has repudiated in a chimera of ideal existence) the very shock of confronting a quixotic self-righteous inwardness out of the heart of the past – the tragic and sterling rebuff administered by my oldest self – makes me discern, in my surrender (or involuntary loss) of an older and clamouring, indignant, exclusive feeling, the truest subduction of slavery into freedom my older self instinctively desired, dissolving every vain attempt one may be driven to make to maintain another unjust cage (either one proud individual measurement or another) for the perfect dead in the undying hope of the living...

I remember the painting of the Battle of Waterloo which hung in my grandfather's drawing-room towards the end of the year 1929. I became aware of it one afternoon in a questionable even treasonable way I had never drawn from within it nor felt upon it before. I was past eight years old then, my grandfather was close to eighty. It happened when the dying (he was then a very ill man though this was a closely guarded secret) Governor of the Colony rode past along East Street. The ghost of a Commander-in-Chief, thin as a reed wearing the glint of glasses like sun on the canal. He held himself painfully (fleshless and upright) in the saddle less like a living man than a shirt cast over branches of rib and bone. His was a dark rock-coloured, still earthen-looking, horse followed by yet another upon which the jerking leaf of a jacket of an orderly fluttered past. It was the Governor's faceless expression in the tree of the sun which stirred in me the picture of a stricken soldier lying on the painted battlefield in my grandfather's sitting-room. And as I stood in the thin throng on the grass-edge of the street to see the grave stick of a personage ride along, there stirred within my mind's eye the painted forest of battle, fallen sculptures carved out of trunks of trees, wearing scarlet flowers of protest on their uniform. I saw the blood of a ruling image (otherwise assumed to be unfeeling and unapproachable as stone) shed on my own familiar homeground. And I began grieving with a singular passion for the unconscious nutriment of freedom however spectral and forbidding it seemed in the long march and funeral procession of figures of conquest.

My grandfather's tenants occupied a tenement range in Waterloo Street – a couple of blocks away from East Street – which I was taken to visit for the first time the day after the Governor rode past. We arrived at the entrance to the property and turned into the brooding alleyway running between two faces of long squat buildings (one reflecting the iron logic of philanthropy, the other meekly bent to the slow unrepentant dream of recovering the coin of profit). I became aware of a living frieze of subjective figures occupying the frame of each doorway in which a group stood or sat with the hollow darkness of their room at their back. It was Saturday afternoon and everyone seemed possessed of the dreadful ease of an unkempt battalion whose economic gratitude and morale were alternatively aroused and shaken as their old landlord paused to address them. The fact was – this fortnightly visit of his (though I did not immediately realize it) was a pure ritual since no one, with the exception of one family of symbolic tenants, the Anthrops, was able to pay a penny of his rent. A slump existed everywhere (a severe retrenchment of investment in the raw materials of business) and the minimum portion of work which could be scraped together within the granite circumstance of the poor went to keep the link of harsh body and charitable soul together.

Nearly all the tenants were six months at least in debt, some had not paid for over a year, and all they could do was continue to plead to be allowed to occupy the rooms at their back into which I now peered, drawn in spite of myself, with the necessity of contemplating a love of horror as if I glimpsed the subterranean anatomy of revolution. *In my Father's house are many mansions*, an underworld, as well, within which might still be bred progenies of change out of the seeming absurdity and perversity of a corner of affection. The old man had no intention of putting them out when he saw they could not pay anything at the moment (unless one knew how to draw blood

46

from stone) but equally he did not intend to relinquish his professional vocation, like a doctor confronting his patient, a commander his troop, to remind them sooner or later their debt of living duty and community must be paid. And there was Anthrop, after all, the head of one family, who miraculously, it seemed, overcame circumstance and settled with him on each occasion he visited. In truth my grandfather was beginning almost to enjoy (though he would never have confessed this) the paradox of it all in the way an artist may grow in awe of the train of his unpredictable material when it becomes capable of the unique momentum of acquiring its own godlike stamp and redeeming character of life.

The family of Anthrop occupied the last couple of rooms in the range: the remainder of the land, extending to a line of paling stakes, stood vacant save for a row of closets and baths in an open net of shadow drawn by the spreading brushwork of leaves from a wide tamarind tree. The occasional dry sweeping fall of leaf and shell caught the outhouses which were crumbling themselves ripe and fast; a bill ruling the latter unfit was soon to be presented to the Legislative Assembly by the Member representing the Municipality. For who would deny that the time had come for every eyesore to be abolished? What profit remained in upholding an art of decay, a canvas of fertile humour, ugly faith, inane, impolitic, thick-skinned, primitive manifesto? Why preserve each brutal wall, judicious hinge, unscientific doorway scored all over by the knife of weather to gape as well as laugh at every patched fruit of initiation into the soil? And yet (wretched economics of nature) here was enthroned the golden centre of inspiration, the most subjective scarecrow earth of all like the religious currency of wood motivated equally by rooted instinct as by growing callouses upon a body of dense spirit leading to an immaterial element of indifference as the quicksilver rain is indifferent to the brightness of the sun. And this treasure of immateriality was the strangest almost undreamt-of experimental thing, a consistency of unrestricted elements within a harsh melting pot of resistances, the crude nature of the sublime long-suffering geography of history.

It was something, however, which in bridging the depth of the mind still leaves one (even after the crossing of many disparate years) vacant and bewildered within a burdensome engagement of prospects. The truth was – in spite of, or because of a natural immunity, fluid raindrop, creative spark – I hated my grandfather's property which seemed capable of turning around in my mind into an unreal triumph over passing time, the relative strength of stable illusion.

I closed my eyes feeling all of a sudden close to sickness: a spinning and sleeping top. The dreaming fit passed. I looked around once again. No one seemed aware that anything had happened. I was subject to these attacks which were accompanied sometimes by spells of vomiting. This time fortunately not. But I experienced once more the resulting chaos I knew, loss of orientation, the unruly pivot around which revolves the abstract globe in one's head. No wonder the mouth of the yard on Waterloo Street seemed to have changed places with its own backside and each legitimate position lay in a contrary direction. This sensation of helpless upheaval, the stigmata of the void, I had first experienced on a Sunday School excursion upriver on which I was forced to go. Seasick, fell asleep, awoke when the boat had turned around and was heading back. We were in sight of the station from which we had originally set out save that the pier under heaven had transplanted itself to the other bank as if to advertise a superior disobedience to the laws of hell: I was in fact obsessed with the idea that I was still travelling *up*, chained to an escort, rather than *down* the river back to where and what I wished...

Anthrop's room had naturally swung with alleyway and corridor. And Anthrop himself appeared at the door wreathed in smiles, full of that unwitting gaiety one associates with the unnatural spirit of the poor. He closed the door quickly behind him to conceal the inmates I had seen: half-naked woman, his wife, with twins at her breast. And my reluctant gaze swung to him with the click of his lock, conferring upon him not the wages of consumption by the new-born but the wages of consumption instead of the new dead. For his face was clearly one of self-reversal of the twins of birth into the hearse-riders whose frightening image of devouring innocence I had obliquely glimpsed.

I came out of hospital at the end of April 1932, scarcely able to credit my own living senses. A moment of brilliant happiness – sun, sheer spirit of illumination, brightest air of freedom. It began with the gloomy notification that I was to stay in for at least another "couple of days" but this injunction was set aside by my step-grandmother whose whirlwind visit overcame the authorities: I was at liberty to go that very morning. After all (they may have given the matter some helpless thought) what difference would it make? There was nothing more they could do. All so quick and abrupt I scarcely credited my good fortune. Liquids still the nurse warned, and it did not seem to matter. What would have been tasteless in hospital became all at once, with the doctor's sentence of release, a capacity of endless enjoyment. I would soon be well and sound again. It was natural I should be led to tell myself so whether anyone else believed it or not. And yet this turned out to be the case. For within a few days the needle within throat and stomach vanished. And left a peculiar stitched taste to grow slowly in the mouth. Not the torn fabric of weakness any longer. The flavour of a curious unexpected patch of despair: tincture (no longer puncture) following just as swift as the incalculable measure of healing and relief… But why then *despair*?

Why now despair (in the self-evident light of thirty-two years of survival) of the successful march and design of life which begins again and again and which began then for *me*? The absolute emphasis, I know, is absurd and yet I still cannot help it after all this time. The stale accumulative fact is I grew miraculously stubborn and strong with each passing hour, passing day, passing season and year, sixteen "explosive" years (only now can I see their inward helpless explosion), twice sixteen of "ebb and flow"… And only now can I begin to penetrate the substance I appeared to gain – the strength of all colourlessness, all hackneyed flavours, the strength to remain within the gratifying spirit of anomaly; not the ghost of freedom I had dreamed I would be, time and time again, in the surrender of everything and every illusion of strength I possessed, but a slave to the futility of hardness, one's everyday conduct, one's everyday meat of existence, one's settlement of helplessness, the fact that one has still not died to it all after all the melted scaffolding of the years (and is only *now* capable perhaps – what self-deception! – of entering into the self-reversing game of reality of the banquet of life on death in one's immortal undiscovered realm, a land of creatures living freely everywhere and nowhere).

The truth is – such apparent delay or procrastination is the tantalizing food of every poor devil's state of eternal convalescence, cruel grace wherein the newly minted appetite of youth acquires the mould of age, a debased currency within which flickers continuously still like a pot on a fire – the thought of being stricken anew by the lightning debt one owes to the weakest inspired beginnings within each vessel of consciousness.

Then indeed, long ago, in the tragic misconceived beginning (one now dreams to return to with a different paradoxical vision of hope) one chose to purchase the manufacture of despair, unwittingly it may be true, and tasted in this bargain a growing hoard of sensibility one conceived as self-sufficient and original, the newfound coin and cement of freedom, instantaneous harvest which seemed truly ambitious, truly right, anything but a miserly or incongruous investment in one's own human prolongation of misery. It had in fact been sown, strange enough, in its own paradoxical expenditure of fire and energy, my sudden all-consuming delight in abandoning a sick bed at a moment's notice which I had not anticipated since I had, in fact, overheard something and was half-prepared to resign myself to the prospect of not only remaining there but never moving out… And then the last thing one had reckoned on happened; I was out in the street of the open world – all thought of dying suddenly forgotten – as if for the first childish profligate time, devouring the burning sweetness of being cooked alive. Home. Relief. Fear soon forgotten, the fear of cruel (only now it seems gentle) death… Thus it was I opened my first proud store of lifeless and lifelike priorities and absurdities and secrets. Yes, I confessed, I was safe and established in my own private being at last. And therefore because of such a conquest of my own space, such a miracle, I dreamed all too rashly (I see it all now) I could never be deprived of my own selfish purchase of reality with each breakthrough into the hidden world at large I knew and desired with a transparent greediness I had never been able to muster before.

L—— came to see me a month after I returned home. We went into the garden which was soft with rain that had fallen overnight and we fashioned figures out of lumps of rich mud.

BOOK TWO

GENESIS

There went up a mist from the earth, and watered the whole face of the ground.

And the Lord God formed man of the dust of the ground…

4

L—— decided to leave when he saw the weather looked uncertain. I accompanied him to the gate with an irrational sensation of a portraiture of disappointment. The air was heavy as the trunk of a tree and the face of the sun was growing into blossom of cloud. It was another instance, I declared, of the bewilderment within each seasonal person and ghostly thing I cherished: the weather of reaction – which had set in very early after my return home continued to demolish each anticipation I had felt springing out of a sense of recovery.

L—— had appeared wooden and unable to enter into the spirit of the game of beginning to make everything new. He looked older than when I had last seen him. I watched him as he broke and moulded the earth and his reluctant, sceptical fingers appeared less capable of strange outer life (I thought a little scornfully in order to depress my own disappointment) than the elongated dead creatures they measured as if their life – the scientific deliberation of his hands – was outside of the phenomenon of dust. They (L——'s hands) were growing to take themselves entirely for granted like implements of un-natural blood.

I loitered by the gate scarcely in the mood to wave to him as he hastened along East Street to catch his bus… At last I turned and began to make my way back to the house; and stopped at the place where he and I had crouched, now scarcely able to believe the thing I created with my own eyes out of one of the pieces he had made and discarded on the ground. For an incredible instant all the sap of life rose anew. I wondered what he would say if he were still here and I were to point to the translated figure and occasion on the ground. I shook my head after a while, slowly, experiencing once again the bewildering pendulum of reaction. Nothing. He would have said nothing and seen nothing. Nevertheless (I shook my head clear again) here was the beginning I sought, the old in the new, whether he was capable of seeing it or sensing it or not. L—— and I (I saw it all within the negative dust which flashed upon my eyes) were to enjoy the enigma of being related... He would acquire a reputation for sober and matchless good sense, judgment, responsibility while I would be the striking unpredictable one. He would never come to blame anyone for the evil which happened to him – as I was often religiously inclined to do – and he would always be restrained, indifferent, in the face of good fortune – as if he could never *see* he deserved any reward which came to him. But even as I counted the measure of his virtues I was conscious that in praising him so highly I was approaching a curious and dangerous subject of apparent generosity and self-satisfaction within myself.

It was all there, the problematic creation and bewildering scale of our lives, in the dutiful expression he had drawn and involuntarily fashioned out of mud as if to make me aware of the surprising and surprised breath of self-critical spirit within his staid and aloof, uncooperative flesh.

The figure which he had made had seemed to me – scarcely five minutes ago – lifeless and unreal. But now the very joylessness with which it had been constructed struck me like a curious revelation of mystical sorrow. I felt cold and strange, a religious stranger to all previous knowledge of emotion; and *emotion* – in such a void or context – became *new*, liberating, oblique, powerless to arouse an expenditure of energy to create the harm I saw I had already inflicted. I could not turn away from the piece which expressed the heart of inarticulate protest in the ground of apparent lifelessness and I asked myself – How did I come to *dream* of one thing and inflict another – the beginnings of such a life of woe on anyone or anything? Was it my impetuous greedy will or L——'s submissive response which seemed to kill one inspiration and feed another? Blobs of breasts, the breasts of mother earth. I came close to laughing – the "dead" figure looked so ridiculously remote from my own flesh-and-blood mother, so unlike that the very distance and unlikeness between the dignity and indignity of her life and the slavishness and imitative mockery of this death stirred a terrifying community and curiosity and an impenetrable need to know whether herein lay the beginnings of the infliction of pain or cruelty on one helpless member by another. Only yesterday it was I was stricken, frozen with astonishment, when I caught a glimpse of my mother's face in a mirror looking like the face of an impossible shadow. Yet it was she, I reminded myself. The door of her room was part open. My step-grandmother and grandfather were addressing her in an ominous persuasive tone and she was weeping bitterly and hollowly, the tears streaming helplessly down her cheeks to mingle like beads of glass in the reflection of her hair. Her fleeting distraught appearance was that of someone in process of being devoured by and in process, too, of devouring a strangled sensation of love. It was the quickest incredible chain of reaction I saw for *they* saw me too and quickly closed the door. There was a silence, the silence within a waterfall when one is suddenly estranged to the music of the self-sufficient senses.

And now the first tinge of nutriment – desire and self-disgust – was born as a shower of rain fell and beads of moisture, the colour of milk, sprouted out of the breast of mud. The mirror of earth and the falling chain grew into a blur as if someone was now veiling herself from the compulsive gaze of instinct; my eyes were torn away from misconceived parent, mesmeric grandparent and step-grandparent into another fold and descending shower of memory – Anthrop's room this time and the naked woman inside, his wife: rolling in fluid procession down the surface of my skin into the corners of my mouth until I felt upon the tip of my tongue the robe of salt. How had the bitter hem of selfish nutriment arrived – did it start by falling from nowhere or was it the native flesh of wisdom within the vehicle of earth? And where did the open fault and dress of inspiration lie which drew every intimate conscription of image into another mourning ancestral cavity standing at one's own tenant's skeleton back?

It was a rainy unstable night following the broken afternoon. Slices of moon now and then appeared like a newborn apparition or the old and declining increment of flesh within a heavy procession of cloud shaped by the dream of my own funeral. The rain ceased to gallop or to shout upon the roof, and the panes of glass in the window glistened, reflecting the transparent assault which had been made upon them. The emotional clamour of the wind – as if the voices of hell itself were let loose – now died down, and the ticking of the grandfather clock within the hall beyond my bedroom door quietly arose growing loud in the new buried silence, uniform and measured, rational and clear.

The sound of the clock was at first distant and somnolent but on gaining one's attentive reflection it developed into something as insistent as everything I had called upon to be made which groaned and protested. Save that its mature and quiet seizure of the stillness of earth now prevailing under the light of the moon led one to dwell with breathless relief upon each erosive trickle of water on the windowpane like a falling minute pendulum pointing to a deeper and ultimate grave of stillness – a creation of silence inhabited by the perfect angelic time of creatures whose presence I dared to hope would outwit all evil and still consent to be shaped by my command and tongue. In dumb animal obedience, a spirit of human (or unhuman) otherness, they would worship and uphold my epitaph and calendar of freedom... I turned on my pillow with a sudden startled moan and a cry I could not suppress. It struck them like an unhappy stroke and they vanished, stripping and unburdening themselves of the slightest trace of clockwork guilt in my order of procession and burial, the pilgrimage of the empire of age back into the colony of youth or – in another sense – the toys of youth obliterated by the march of age I had unwittingly imposed on them; retreating even deeper into their dialogue of genesis.

They were my dreaming instinctive models, Angels (sometimes capable of recall, sometimes elusive and sealed and forgotten) of childhood and ageless transformation, the sword over the garden and the tomb – mother earth L—— had pretended to consent to make, and the wages of self-mockery Anthrop had pretended to enjoy.

The Night of self-initiation, self-kinship, grew into celestial furniture, the great hearse rolled on, stitched planks held by the scissors of the universe, divisions of cloud within which glimmered the operations of space; the moon had been pared right down to lie almost like a needle upon a backcloth of stars: I saw the flagged pathway flutter and roll before me backwards and forwards and backwards until the sheet unwound itself into a stream of cotton, the rippling surface of the bedclothes of East Street canal... The rough-hewn figure of Anthrop descended from beside his dwarf of shadow. The seat of his trousers shone like milk in the frailty of the moon, it was so worn, threadbare if not fleshbare. It was his custom to come once a month to trim my grandfather's nightmare toenails. Sometimes it was a solemn function but often it was merely a duty he performed as with the march of each clown or corpse he drove, and that was why he often joked and laughed in a blunt, even rude, fashion with his idol of a landlord... On this occasion an unexpected thing happened when he arrived. Halfway along the framed carpet running to the sleeping picture of the house he encountered someone who was the spit and image of himself, cast from an identical yet deceptive mould. It was Anthrop's twin brother who had risen high even as Anthrop had fallen low.

They passed each other with the barest flicker of a nod, a grain of thread on the forehead of my bedpost, Anthrop, the rude unnatural one, and Anthrop the rich civil engineer.

In the needle's eye of light Anthrop's twin resembled not so much his crude brother but a gentler and younger frame as well: *this was L——'s father, I swore, no one else*. I half-groaned, half-laughed. It was a joke in poor taste. Why resurrect such a shameful scandal? Poor L——. It was rumoured that his dead mother (L—— was an orphan) was still in love with engineer Anthrop, in fact had always been his secret mistress.

Even as I *dreamed* I was aware of a bewildered protest I tried to express. I wanted to protest against an incredible logic where all frontiers refused to collapse into each other – innocent prejudice into guilt, death and its unbroken assumption into a new life, motion into the flight of stillness. How could she – the dead mother of the living fatherless child – live and move with such resurrected constancy and inconstancy in my dreaming mind, remaining nevertheless subject to the same laws of censure and propriety, self-hatred and self-love? Would Anthrop's rich successful brother always exist in no other form for her (and for me) but that of being her illegitimate lover, my assumption of twin scandal and bankruptcy, the family of the void, loveless eternity, solipsis, love's own extremity?... But even as I struggled to find a way of new conviction other than the ancient riddle of protest I knew the changeless ground of it all would yield ultimately, of its own accord, when it succeeded in marrying the fearful strength of the past to the infant freedom of choice which was still weak in the conviction of the present and the future: my own impulsive rein of eagerness and repulsive light of action grew brutally fitful and restrictive as the uncertain spring of day – I was *pushing* her (I was aware of a contrary rebuke and stillness in the heart of crude action) – *pushing* her, nevertheless, even as I had involuntarily pushed him, her son, into the canal and to the brink of his (and her) total self-acceptance, total responsibility for my bewildered self belonging to both sides of the blanket, illegitimate one of present speculation and legitimate reinforcement to escape from the prison of past knowledge.

I found myself pushing her into the streaming bedclothes and into my own cupboard and skeleton of shadow – the ghost on the gallows I had once shuddered to see in the mirror of the canal but whose spiritual reflection I now assured myself would bring her no living harm. While it would do me a great service by accepting my dead burden of fright, legitimate or illegitimate, by consenting – without caring – to suffer my technical goad and translation which was consistent, after all, with the daily caress and instrument of callous love.

I pushed her and she fell into these uninspired arms, the engineer of depth, and dissolved into the scaffold of one drowned reflective self to my sudden indescribable horror. I heard myself shout (though scarcely able to believe my own ears) that it was all my fault, plunging forward before it was too late to pull her out and draw her up into my own gauge of budding self-deception, self-knowledge and hanging extremity, my illusion of freedom. She rose and I was established in *him*, in his phallic technical right, the dead man's living right, thereby abolishing the necessity for him at one stroke. (*The news arrived yesterday that her engineer had been drowned – the police were investigating…*) I turned away from his subjective memory to fulfil our mutual engagement: *but it was my own mother – and no scapegoat of woman – who had come into the room and was lying beside me.* I had given such a great cry she had come to console me. She, too, had been weeping over the black news of yesterday. *I cried again on waking to find her beside me – It isn't true.* What? she asked. But my tongue refused to budge or plead. I couldn't utter the thing aloud, the significant conversion of every dumb fact: and that in this unrestricted silent conversion lay the retrenched and elusive and invincible principle of a pure timeless kinship with…

The almost unendurable unity, silence and sacrifice, de-

61

parted; and I was able to voice an individual borderline existence of fear with a sense, nevertheless, of having glimpsed,
however obscurely, implications of the breakdown of nightmare rule.

So it was I jumped forward into an echoing future (which is
now with the dead voices of the past) and into a middle of a year
– a great procession – the striking year of every man's familiar
obsession (1948 or 2048?). L—— and I suddenly stumbled
upon the faint but "timeless" footprints of a *self-created* self –
the stepfather for whom my mother wept (as if she had been
weeping for *me* as well as for *him* all the time).

She had mourned long (years which wear centuries and
centuries of disguise operated upon afresh by instigators of
memory to probe an endless frustration and desire) hoping
against hope he would still return until the news arrived that he
had been drowned in the heart of the interior. I recalled him
vaguely. I remembered the time he conducted me around the
garden on a bicycle: I was five years old; it was all so faint and
curiously disagreeable in my mind I dreamt to cut him from us
altogether and to divest her of the burden of such an unreal and
yet cruel dragging presence.

But in this lawful (or was it unlawful?) persuasion I failed
and his life remained a millstone of responsibility: he had set
foot into the past in search of proof of another's (or was it my
own?) disfigured innocence. When the news came of his
certain death by drowning – it was then a full month since my
return home from hospital – it had seemed that *now* the
obscure trial of all time was over. And yet the circumstances
remained like an absurd chain drawing one up into the depths
of the future and down into the image of the past.

It was this depth of recognition I feared, seeing – in this – the
anticlimax of the universe continuously reflected, the law of an
unlawful beginning and a lawless end, and of beginning all over
again without end, a curious ill-defined substitute for someone

else I had never known and whom it would have been easy to erase from consciousness were it not that one faint persistent searching memory stirs the other sleeping shape and dust: I was thinking of the tragic indistinct life of my actual parent and father – tragic I knew with the yearning bones of instinct – who died, it was reported, when I was less than a minute old...

L—— was the engineer in charge of the expedition to the lost womb of a mining town, nine months' journey from Water Street into the jungle of conception traversed along each changing river of ascent; the same scale of measurement emerged when taken from each accumulative deposit of memory in the garden east of Waterloo to the heights of Sorrow Hill.

I stood on a suspension bridge overlooking an arm of the river, conscious of Sorrow Hill at my back: a ripple, a footprint almost, appeared in the middle of the water and vanished. I stood still and waited. The sun shone with an unbending matchless stroke. Neither a feather of wind nor a fin of cloud now moved. They waited, too, for the huntsman of death to return, the hunter to become the hunted. It was a strange inviting and yet curiously uninviting thought. Watching, listening: the body of the stream ceased to breathe, growing still as the mound of sleeping sand, the contours of which I saw, fiery and distinct, in the middle of the river; in fact the river over the sand bank was a glittering shell and enclosure, a coffin of transparency, skeleton-key deep, the colour of its shallow bed like the hot blast of snow. The dazzling sleeper of spirit, exposed within the close elements, the refraction and proximity of sun and water, awoke all too suddenly and slid, in a flash, like speechless gunfire, from crown to toe, along the slowly reddening whiteness of the sand, turning darker still like blood as it fell; and ultimately black as the river-bottom descended, vanishing into a ripple, a dying footfall again, darting across the deep roadway of water and rising once more, distinct web or trace of animation upon a flank of stone.

L—— saw nothing of this and yet I could not help feeling as I turned to him that *it*, the trespass of feeling rising anew out of the stumbling labour and melting pot of history, had also touched him however indirectly or obscurely. His manner remained cool but I believed he was still deeply moved: he was pointing to the engineering merits of the bridge, the excellence and height of the site, the outcrops of rock in which the steel cable on either side was embedded. My stepfather had done a remarkable job he declared. And he wondered whether he would be able to do the same. (I myself was staring into the river and I wondered if it was upon the very plank on which I stood *he* had been trapped, *stunned*). The execution was perfect, L—— said. The remark struck me in a flash: I gave an incredible start (as if I had been immersed very deeply, thinking, but *not* of my stepfather's bridge at all) and pulled my gaze away from the water. The bridge was both a trapdoor and a poem. We had seen it from another angle yesterday, several miles away downriver and it appeared like the most fragile and beautiful web against the sky. The first enduring superstitious bastion which a spider of science had spun against the inroads of the jungle, appeared symbolically to overcome its own erosive empirical faculty and slender truth.

It was no use disclosing my thoughts to L——. His face was growing blank, devoid even of the slight hanged trace of emotion I had glimpsed. And I – as a consequence – was flooded with the kind of awe he inspired in me on certain occasions, the sheer and limitless power of retrenchment I visualized which was capable of stirring the most profound, almost inexpressible residues of feeling.

It was on my suggestion he had sent for a woman from the ghost of the mining town some miles upriver. But when she arrived I shrank inwardly from her and could not bring myself to touch her. It was the grossness of her breasts and the enormity of her buttocks. L—— did not sense this and when I asked him how he had got on with her he looked at me with his blank look as if he had not attempted to strip her at all, had been content merely to penetrate through everything, clothing, flesh, hair and gristle, with a blind and instinctive precision, a total acceptance of his responsible and her unalterable necessity, which made her naked compliance the most riddling factor of all. However ugly, however grotesque, she remained a fact and therefore a mystery. The thought of such unimaginable boundless freedom, such a paradox of extension born of the limitless subduction of everything within an essential activity, made my head spin. I clung in desperation to the rail of the bridge though it was falling into the river's snow and sun.

5

The clearing which had been made in the jungle where the suspension bridge spanned the river drew one to crane one's neck back in order to experience a measure of blind relief – the height and depth of the sky – as if this alone, the uncovering of inner space, would overcome an approximate void in sensation one felt in spinning to a groundless fall. The *daemon* I now felt rising within such an open relationship to understanding the baselessness of sensation, was drawn to inhabit an insubstantial premise of cloud, sailing over the harbour of earth to a wider settlement and bay, trailing a rope of shadow which now gradually stretched and lengthened across the seeming gulf of incompatible reality: the flag of the sun was upheld by a broomstick of rain. Brushes of shadow were augmented by a coil of leaves rising fast to sweep the top of the forest. I had closed my eyes but I saw the muse of place descending hand over hand along the jointed rope and stick of the atmosphere.

The presence which appeared to settle within the gloom beneath me was actual I knew, but I equally knew it was folly to open my eyes and look. It might prove to be someone I loathed or despised – a base ugly trick of the matted senses: and if no one really existed I was bound to founder or wilt, of my own accord, in the self-deceptive voyage of exploratory nature.

Either way would be an absurd defeat for the true knowledge I dreamt I embraced and possessed. Scarcely moving I now felt encircled by another's rising flesh, a moving trunk, violent arms and legs, and I bowed the column of my neck at last, remaining blind nevertheless to the end, releasing myself – with the thought I had truly and deeply endured belonging to the other (as the other had truly and deeply endured belonging to me) – from the cable and rail to which both of us still clung like tendrils of flesh to a shaft of bone.

L—— was oblivious to either pillow of air or monument of fantasy. He, too, had been craning his neck backwards, nevertheless, I dreamed, pointing sightlessly to a certain tension in the nervous wires overhead and explaining to me with mute detail the distribution of load which was capable of moving upon and occupying the deck of the bridge. His voiceless witness faded from my head as if it and I had never existed. I slept and awoke and she (*the prostitute from the mining camp*) was still lying beside me. It was I indeed who had penetrated her with borrowed force and intensity as she had held me and enveloped me within the rule of passion. I could not bring myself to turn and look at her – as at the *hideousness* of all apparent charm.

But even as I turned away from her I was conscious of the jealous furious ground of instinct: I had sparked her into feeling that sheer beauty or ugliness was a fearful myth which neither L—— nor I would ever dare to face: such a gust of emotion I felt, it drew from me in turn a curious sigh, the genesis of hostility towards him. As if I could not help seeing in him my own folly laid bare at last, the emergency and divide inspired by her, his whore within the blind lust we sought, each of us, to perpetrate upon her, all alone, without conceiving of the shameful (or shameless) existence of another. It was the most difficult trial and conviction for me to begin to accept the unpalatable truth that we – who sought to make her our plaything – were her maternal joke as well (twins of buried and divided fantasy) and that a price was about to be placed upon our heads which would involve us – whether we wished it or not – in the breath of unfamiliar origins, familiar genius – in the soul of something she desired to *see*, and was prepared to nurse into existence by fair means or foul: the restoration of her spiritual bridge and sacred mining town.

L—— was protected – in the stable right of his profession – from the growing consequences of the endless goal of rehabilitation: it was never a matter of proud selfish appetite with him (whatever indifference his appearance may have reflected) or cruel self-flattery to the point of an extinction of all else. I was not however so protected (and in truth had never been) by blind innocent nature as he quite simply was. My horror of corruption and longing for vocation remained. And I began to discover a force of obsession in things I had only dimly dreamt before (it seemed to me now) to question, things and persons I had accepted too easily (it seemed now, once again) for what they were supposed to be and what they were instinctively supposed not to be. Things and persons whose life of obsession lay less within themselves and more within myself, within my lack of a universal conception, of their conception (the unborn folk). Less in the open question of their apparently submissive being and more in my ultimatum of fixed instincts, beyond which – the residual fire or magnetic field of which – I hesitated to go (even dared not go) since it would mean crossing a "dead" masked frontier as if this were a living disguise and territory in fact…

This was the first obstinate difficulty we encountered in attempting to locate the ancient trails to the ghost town. L—— decided to open a trail in the forest but the bearing he chose to follow was distorted on his compass by a magnetic instinctual load of rock in our neighbourhood. We abandoned the line, pored over the uncertain mirror of our maps, and brought the woman once more in to the picture. She was reputed to know the reflection of the country like a dog its shadow of bone. I accused her of misdirecting us and she gesticulated and pointed in all directions, needling us but apparently failing to sting us in the way she wished as if our flesh had turned to wood. *It was all our fault, our void, disorientation*. Hebra her name was, as unlikely a name as the Queen of the South (some of the dead miners of the ghost town had once so nicknamed her). RAVEN'S HEAD. She spat this name at us like the dreadful severance of reflex and afterthought. Anything to make us *jump* in answer to the knife-edge of destiny. L—— was jotting each bearing down, cool as water, without the blink of a stony eyelash, anything he could glean which might prove a useful pointer later on. It was I who had urged him to accept the leadership of the engineering expedition – I wanted to claim and protest. But this seemed so pointless now (I had never been so jealous of my freedom and his authority before): how could I reasonably protest against, or on behalf of, something which was much more and so much less than any vision of responsibility I had hoped to puncture and entertain?

For centuries, everyone darkly knew, mysterious locations had been plumbed to disappear and return once more into the undisclosed astronomical wealth of the jungle. *Raven's Head* – by which name Hebra herself was sometimes known – Hebra's town – was one of these relative establishments whose life of eternity sprang from a pinpoint conception of poetic loyalty to the idea of everlasting justice: they (such relative establishments) belonged to those who voluntarily began to relinquish the right they deserved to a place in them – whose recovery of them lay therefore within the heart of an acceptance of great distance from them. But such a decision to relinquish what one desperately wanted to find tore at the roots of all possession and conventionality. How could I begin to endure the thought that it was I who may have instigated such an unendurable search and undemonstrable claim? No wonder my protest was stifled at the outset within the inadequacy of jealous proprietorship and conviction, the arid frame of past ruling justice or sentiment. The memory of such ruling sentiment – still undivorced from possession or place – threatened to choke me afresh, sediment rather than sentiment, the sediment of abortive constellations – the hanged man's noose over Hebra's town – within whose dry brittle air one distantly perceived the almost breathless fall of the condemned blossom of earth – the freedom of promise in dust; the very dusty insects were drawn to flight: their infinite grind and procession capable now of aerial relief. Each wall or door carved on their backs fell into the stars, disappeared in truth yet were driven to await one's logical chain of delayed recognitions of the fact. A thousand years in our sight to earn a moment in theirs. The moment of our transplantation, the conception of our roots pinpointed in their mainstream...

And yet in spite of my knowledge of the truth, indeed because of this – the very apparent helplessness of dwindling truth – my rage for self-justification knew no bounds. I was forced for the first time to cry out against my own patient role of inheritance. *My father is no murderer*, I cried (no longer able to suppress the retrenched ground of emotion). *There are records in Raven's Head which will prove he was framed* and... I caught my breath... EXECUTED. Why was it – in spite of insubstantial time and eternity – the transience of everything – I still could not utter and abolish the long-standing self-injurious word of sentence? My tongue was turning to stone rather than confess to something so infamous and baffling which I had seen stitched across the years, my unlicensed censor of space. I saw the veiled silent reproof and mocking question on Hebra's black mask of a face which rose between L―― and me: she stood like a jagged daughter of cloud in the light of the moon now shining just above our shoulders; the

69

shoulders of Sorrow Hill. All at once I dreamed that *it* – the accumulative ironies of the past, the virtuous rubbish-heap and self-parody of ancestors in death – still sought to warn me not to dig into itself so deep for the classical burden of truth (I was thinking, without clearly realizing it, of my grandfather's solid puritan instinct to dismiss the collective ghost – especially when it arrived as my outlaw and his heir, agnostic barrier and still essence of science and art and love – I was influenced as well by my mother's reflection embodied within an unreasoning tradition of fear: fear that my unwelcome (stepfather's?) attachment to her (was it true or not that he had been my own father's engineering colleague and friend?) may have compelled him – in order to win from the family of his adoption their everlasting gratitude and affection – to leave his well-ordered camp and *plunge* into the closed forbidden jurisdiction of the past in search of my open gauge and sceptical grain of fact...)

It wasn't proof of a father's innocence or a stepfather's adventure into the vanishing point of pork-knocker law and justice L—— was after. He didn't give an orphan's damn for this. He had been commissioned to relocate Raven's Head because it was now suspected – fifteen or twenty years after its disappearance – that fantastic gold deposits lay in the river thereabouts. The difficulties were rich and enormous. A needle in the rubble of a haystack. In the first place it was uncertain whether the Raven's Head he sought lay on this river or twenty-five stitched jangled miles away on the next. (There were *two* Raven's Heads according to oral tradition.) In the second place not only did these mushroom settlements spring up overnight, they disappeared as rapidly, and often attempts at particular relocations had to face the fact that rash new mining premises were shooting up still, here and there, each claiming to cloak an original site. This tradition and confusion of forms proved often to be the wreck of all hope for a recovery of an original nucleus of villages.

70

L—— knew it was imperative to do an extremely careful job in respect of Raven's Head. For his principals were contemplating an astronomical investment, labour, machinery, a new township. Once they were thoroughly satisfied they would set about establishing dredging operations in the section of the river beneath the original village and these would be accompanied by drilling work as well on both banks.

If they could not find the Raven's Head they sought they would naturally be compelled to abandon the project or to embark on expensive, possibly fruitless, prospection of the whole difficult and uncertain area.

It was no use stirring a nail to transport the parts of the dredge until they were certain they had located (and tested) their actual claim on the ground which existed on government parchment all the time. (L—— shook his head – as if he wanted to brush my cobwebs and complaints aside – when I spoke to him of probing the irresponsible legality of such licences and deceptive records.)

The war had reduced all conventional communications to paper transport services, lorry and truck – L—— spoke apologetically as if by way of parable – to a standstill. And even before that there had been upheaval, feud and misery, the disruption of the self-evident normal passage of events. It was curious but he referred to the war as if it was associated with some kind of native reflex, his generation of earthquake (the implication, perhaps heretical, which arose in my mind – as he spoke – pointed to an ancient trail which was an apprehension of live response beyond the fixed limit he imposed on a residual society): an action for which no one – beyond a certain self-appointed region – stood to blame, L—— insisted – as though he read my mind and saw he could not remove the nagging seal of doubt. And if indeed any further blame was necessary, the misjudgment or misconception of reality – he agreed – then *he* – because of his insusceptibility to a continuing motion or cause outside of himself (or, in other words, because of his susceptibility to himself as his own faulty agent) – must suffer the blame, in terms of his own absolute logic of context, solely, in the numb fixture of himself. He was trapped within the riddle of his own leaden machinery – the riddle of the fixed instincts.

At such moments of absolute prejudice and resistance – within and without – immobility – L—— struck me as the advocate of the devil of humility in himself: he became the insensible nature of dreaming relationship to guilt and absurdity, the most ancient of convictions, and the most modern of sciences – empirical responsibility (and lack of responsibility) I wrestled with day and night: he fulfilled the most negative role of all – the self-imposed ratification of every closed sentence I could not truly accept and which I found myself helplessly probing in order to uncover wherein lay the movement of original compassion, the furthest point and agency of reason and the source of an active responsible *spiritual* (L—— loathed the word) tradition still.

There was one poorly constructed road running up from the coast (L—— spoke again in his unreflective way and without a germ of reproach, pointing to a map of creatures as though *it*, in truth, had no living existence) and this was in a state of almost universal neglect.

The job of moving the dismantled giant armature of the dredge, bolt by bolt, rib by rib (if the project should once be set in motion) would lie – for a time at any rate – on the slender back of what personal initiative in river transportation was available: a herculean task but not impossible. It would fall upon creatures of little weight and substance, this was true, (L—— spoke now as if he had come around, in the end, to humouring me out of some obscure necessity) legs and paddles and arms, Captain Funeral Fetish – the *one* of innumerable generations – and his fellow tenants of the bush, half-insect, half-animal, crawling in procession on the watertop and along every scant portage around the falls and rapids. In short – L——

was half-joking, half-sad, a confession amounting almost to self-defeat – there was small certainty the mission he had accepted would be successfully accomplished and *seen* to be established in his (or its?) own self-sufficient terms.

BOOK THREE

RAVEN'S HEAD

Sister and wife at once; for without the use of the body
Mentally she unites, for the Spouse is God, not a man.
    Out of this mother is born the Ancient as well as the
infant…

PAULINUS OF NOLA

*The Eye*s

Closed, they are waiting. Open, they're also waiting.
They are acquainted,
but they have forgotten the name of their acquaintance.

TENNESSEE WILLIAMS

6

The horse was trotting amiably along Water Street when suddenly – without the slightest warning – it reared; neighed stridently. The respectable-looking carriage it drew lurched and appeared to be toppling on its side when it narrowly righted itself. The driver descended from his high box, held the dream-ridden horse by the reins, and began reassuring him. The horse seemed to possess a sinister memory and yet still to respond – out of a grateful and fearful desire – to the human, if not divine hand upon its neck and head. It was the custom in these parts for horses to wear shades against their eyes which allowed them to see straight ahead, up or beneath but never from side to side so whatever it was had frightened the creature may have passed right under or above its nose and then beyond the cloak of sight.

An old man and a young boy sat inside the carriage. They, too, like the supernatural driver and the supernatural horse belonged to this and every age of an insufficiency of vision. They came out into the street looking bewildered and blindfolded themselves. It was a still flowing night all around them they did not appear to see. Sightless they may have been like the bright lid of the street light overhead which had acquired a curious halo of flying insects, out of which unbroken circle every now and then a pair of wings flew straight at the vulnerable pilot of flame which revealed itself to be less vulnerable than imagined; its own alert and deadly and protective skull of a transparency like glass.

The incident occurred within a stone's throw of the ancient and modern riverwall, and the timeless river stood waiting to be discerned like a dark floating ball on which the lighted shadow of its own interior had formed itself into ships whose cargo was no less than the motion of the earth.

It was impossible to say what had startled the cryptic head of the horse. Its hide crinkled and shuddered and trembled all over and through its beaked eyes there issued a rolling and endlessly perturbed glance.

The driver endeavoured to calm its affright so that the carriage might proceed but without success. The horse stood as if riveted to the ground: with its head flung back and its presence against the river and the sky, it acquired both the illumination and the fringes of shadow inherent in Night – an extraordinary witness of Raven's Head gate or barrier. It was turning into its own forbidding gateway on the North, the Gateway of Fear.

There were, after all, four possible approaches to Raven's Head town sometimes called Hebra's Town: Raven's Head Gate on the north, Hebra's Gate on the south, the Suspension Bridge on the west and Sorrow Hill on the east. And these approaches were ceaselessly inclined to grow blurred and insensible to their origins – to be drained as it were of all consciousness of all dialogue with the emotion or genius of place and to become outcrops of common mud or stone shaped by the indifferent hand of the dead god of the seasons into an arrested weathercock.

On all sides a siege was laid to the *will*, the will to go forward until one's resolve became – caught in its own paradox – the fortress of environment. The ancient gun which had once boomed at the gateway of the Demerara fort on the riverwall was now silent: silent as a dream of infant thunder in the heart of Sorrow Hill, a silence which was both the mature issue and the startled product of a crippled role and inborn struggle anew for comprehension within incomprehension.

Morning and night for a century or more the great gun used to shake the primitive approaches to the city and it was at such an early or late pregnant hour – though it had long ceased to fire as in the commanding years before – the horse and carriage of the Ancient of Days stopped and responded: a permanent fixture or capture this was which had nevertheless been transported into the interior, elsewhere and everywhere, appearing equally fixed – the late mental door and early battering ram of besieger and besieged.

It was – in spite of the universal predilection for waging symbolic war – a totally different ornamental approach if one sought to enter the lost town by rediscovering Hebra's Gate. It had always been, even in the best of years, a difficult problem to keep this unpredictable door and roadway open to the traffic of work-ridden and travel-ridden vehicles crawling like nightmare motorized infantry against the endless density and abstraction of space on earth. The ghosts which paraded were equally reminiscent of mechanical age and youth though it was most difficult to say who was captor and who captive. No image of respectable fantasy existed here: neither stately procession nor horse nor carriage; the landscape was genuinely wild in a manner which seemed to lay bare the true and darkest intimate recesses of the life of proliferate nature, the life of the born jungle against the life of a disintegrating tribal society.

There were even expanses along the variable road – like stitched cloth of grass within a hostile though withdrawn brooding encirclement – where the tribal shepherd appeared still intact. The grazing spirits of his cattle sometimes broke the fences and crossed the open road hereabouts, seeming still almost totally oblivious to the sudden possible acceleration of enemy traffic. In fact everything depended on the alien driver's reflex or invading clutch of instinct, the fluid brake of all vehicular times present to him, to save them (and himself from running them down) in a stationary past which was all that was present to them. The mooning cows spent an age in their slow exasperating walk from one eternal parapet to another reflecting their own archaic memory of address and landscape where

79

the surviving march of ridge or valley was infinitely retarded, infinitely slow. The volcanic pace of everything subsided within a certain reduction of the span of lightning consciousness into an obsolescent earthborne sleep which came close to recapturing the dreamless clarity and innocence of a babe in an antique cradle. Within such a slow almost totally withdrawn figure of progress the animal of fate and patience learnt to move: its advantage over the horse, dream-ridden horsepower, gear, clutch, brake and driver, lay in its insusceptibility to the nerves of both flight and fear. It never actually ceased to move across its pedestal, however indifferently and still slowly, in response to its own scale of proportion and attunement, the universal arrested diaphragm of every glaring landslide; and with this unerring statuesque degree of just motion the animal's head lifted, swung *now*, *deliberately*, to address the oncoming rush and menace of an approaching machine: something which was – in the eye of the sacred cow of Raven's Head – truly lacking in all swift exposure, instant credibility, substance or dread.

But (and it was the first time the driver of the machine was deceived) a misconception arose which remained implacably framed in the mind of place – the *Inn or Resthouse of the Quartering of the Cow* – one of a number of signs pointing to the ancient mining town. *He* (the driver) was certain the animal had swung its head in order to turn and sidle to the left as well as back the way it had come. It was an elementary manoeuvre, he felt, and the equilibrium and assurance of the beast made it appear obvious and inevitable. Furthermore a certain self-confidence in his own eye of judgment – room and place – had been paradoxically aroused a moment ago, when shortly before he drove out of the twilight encampment of the jungle into the shepherd's clearing he had discerned the tigercat of the bush. The tiger – known in this locality as deer-tiger – the "cat with the devil's horns" – was dressed as always in her deceptive gentle reddish brown coat. Her eyes however were naked in their own fierce right. The instant she spotted the driver upon her, there was a flash of lightning, vibration, tuning-fork, *spring*, the plucked harp of motion, *gone*. She had vanished and all that remained was the thunder of his own gasp and response. It was as if the earth had opened and swallowed her and the intervening light void of black consciousness, the open tumult of everything, nervous precipice, vicarious *impact*, death (for though she had escaped he almost dreamed he had hit her) landfall, waterfall, were all reduced to incomprehension and vast silence. Out of which emerged an inflation of *his* not *her* achievement, the certainty that it was *he* who had seen *it* and skilfully avoided all.

The balloon of false reaction led straight to the roots of premature self-assurance and conviction. Far from sidling back to her side of the road, the cow, that incredibly slower beast, continued to march forward. It was too late for him to stop or for her to change her hide and escape. The mortal blow she received was like a shattering of his own barrier of stupidity and indifference and predictable image.

The closed structure of Will, the fortress of environment, had parted. The old man (clothed now in shepherd's rags) and his grandson were tending the driver of the machine. The vehicle itself was smashed: it had collided with a curious half-feminine, half-bovine obstruction. The uncertain road through the jungle was strewn with these numinous boulders.

The driver had had a miraculous escape and he was soon recovered sufficiently to accept a portion of the shepherd's evening meal. This had been prepared out of boiled plantains which were then crushed to pulp in a mortar with a pestle. The brown fatty mass which emerged was considered delicious: one could discern pale minute flecks of the original fruit or vegetable substance, which had escaped being ground, like the perfect iota of shell sprinkled here and there.

From the running ball of conversation between grandfather and grandson the driver was able – in spite of an apparently phlegmatic disposition which may have been professional and native or on the other hand the stunned immediate consequences of responsibility for his every collision – to visualize his own flight (blind passage of pitfall and footfall which lay ahead of him).

No use walking or driving or riding with one's head in the clouds. *He* (the driver) was only too well aware of this. He did not need grandfather and grandson to tell him so. But their presence had emerged upon a frontier of existence which was involved with the exploratory fact of his freedom or unfreedom, authority or lack of authority. Should self-deception (it was a thought he of all persons had never properly faced before) – in its most intimate paradox of a practical heaven of reality – fall to his lot, it was precisely because of his own acquiescence to stunned premises, the kind of engineered space in which he bargained to rule himself – and be ruled by himself – by allowing of no sensible proportion except in his own standing or stumbling experience of it. And for this reason he did not know how to begin to accept the possibility that he was being counselled or pushed, wittingly and unwittingly, fairly and unfairly, by someone and something other than himself whether apparently conservative and old or revolutionary and young.

And yet – now for the first time he was not so sure. The counsellors of past and present generations might possess – in the midst of the fruitless noises of conflict they appeared to make, the abracadabra of gesture and sound – an element of indistinct dialogue which survived within their vociferous arts of force and persuasion. Had it become vital to listen and look to them more carefully and acutely than he had ever listened and looked to anyone attending him before?

The apparent depth and horror of his position dawned on him. He felt a sharp agonized division – a sensation of being drawn convulsively *up* as well as pulled instantly *down* into the bodily (or bodiless) mystery of mysteries he dreaded: a way he had not conceived himself experiencing in a present or a future; the flock of himself – animal substitute, strung-up, reflective – stood unnaturally poised within the conjunctive witness of another eye, a window within and without both shepherd and friend, ancestor and legend – the utterly re-trenched and flashing instinct of the purest severance and witness of a consciousness of mute self-revolving parts in endless dialogue.

The very clearing into which he had been driven or had stumbled appeared now to have settled into an involuntary hole in the ground. It was marked by a certain intelligence it had taken him ages it seemed to discover, a burrowing re-sourceful intelligence he had been unable to stop himself from overlooking – methodical it now looked, secretive, too – layer by layer, starting with the heavy air and overgrowth of his feeling and descending into their lighter soil through different grains and lines of featureless texture and textureless feature. The iron trunk of a tree fallen from above emerged far beneath like the lantern skull of gloom. Did the shepherd's night of overcast passage and cottage stand upon one of the lost captive lighted foundations of fear of an upper world – the world to which he (the driver) apparently and solely belonged? The driver of the broken machine laughed at himself for being an aimless fool. He was turning – or falling – into the pool or thoroughfare of someone both like and unlike himself.

He and the other – unlike and like – stood almost face to face, yet – miserable banner of all ages – masked at the same time, horse or tiger, animate cow or brute stone, sovereign or primitive device. Both were intent, beyond conventional enve-lope and address, on penetrating the other's vulnerable (or was it invulnerable?) carriage of secrets. Each one surmised the other's ideal stamp or picturesque emotive flag of animal landscape was clothed with danger and design, the danger of being confounded by immortal purpose and mislaid in the process by a postman or nightmare servant of design: while at the same time there stood as well the promise of a delayed telegram – movement towards the cradle of fulfilment – indistinct holes, pockmarks, monosyllabic crude lettering and utterance, canals and rivers descending into the cottage or ship of space from a projection of the moon, still rising and running forwards or backwards (no one could say which) *into* or *out of* the macroscopic script of Water Street and Ferry Road on this individual map, harbour and historical planet. (Such a tidal record of legend and impression – involving absurd codes of memory, inflation, as well as the acute thorn and nib of painted humility – witnessed to the porous skin of all oversize frontiers on earth which were drawn to gather themselves into hypothetical island or universe or pool upon the most ancient flesh of manuscript: herald and chart of precipitation, ground-plan of every modern and tribal entrepot, proud leaf of gravity adorned by names of delivery and adventure.)

Who was the engineer of such revolving barrier, despatch and arrest (birth and death) and where (or how) had it been possible to manufacture, for all eternity, in each self-important blocked device, the minuscule fleet of soul and necessary solution of origins?

It was the question one asked as though each invited the other to surrender his currency and ink of offspring, bloody password into the dark room of noble and ignoble execution, bunk of ocean, pilot and postmaster of buried access to unholy freedom, each one felt the other knew and stored for the purest selfish locked reasons.

Such a question drew one into the other's corridor of secret even treacherous mode of contemplation, the giant of place against whose enveloping, broad, plain countenance one stood so close as to lose the vision of him and indeed everything save that there existed a miniature almost forgotten universal stamp in the mind – the seal of the hanged dwarf of God. No longer were the foundations of the open city a great smashed subverted machine, destined to be anchored and helpless in time, but a rifled envelope at worst, still bearing the inner privilege of communicating with a true signature of parts…

It came as a shock to the dreamer to find that the barrier which had stopped him was thin as paper, a logical stamp like a breath of air, suspended portrait, thumbprint, ghostly reflex. That it possessed such stubborn strength, such enduring power born of extension out of the catastrophic past, was the nature of the dilemma confronting the emotional dynamics of reason. It would be an admission of defeat to stop and consent to be thwarted by a bridge of obsession, the web of spirit. It was up to him, his conviction being what it was, to go forward into the future. And this was a strange uneasy way of putting the case, *his* case, after all. What conviction was it which had been propelling him and marshalling him all along in spite of everything? He resented the echo of such naïveté, intuition, call it what one will, and of mystical forces drawn up in retrospective battle array on a private or public ancestral front. It was all bound up with such frightful and undying exploits of spiritual conscience and absurdity… He was an engineer and he practised and held himself totally responsible for an abstract form of measurement, control. It was – he paused and relented a little, standing on the verge of conceding a point to his opponent – perhaps indeed it could be described, in all fairness, as a conviction. But the tribunal or theatre of action, court-room, arena, living-room, bedroom, saloon, highway (the names of conviction and habit were legion) was one which it was his job solely to plan or build afresh in all emergencies in more or less precise, even though apparently mathematical, obscure, dented or insufficient material terms. It was the utilitarian spirit of improvement and responsibility which led him. But this was, once again (he knew he must watch himself) going too far. Nothing was leading him or had ever led him. Might as well say and blame inspiration for everything that happened. How could *he* – after all – be subject to such a crumbling mode of pointlessness and uncertain vagary of instinct? Could such an alien residue of motivation, outside of his proper intention, propel him beyond the ultimate marginal self-conception he held – the architect and engineer of the immediate framework of society – into discoveries of past and future associations he never dreamt of fashioning into solid residence and existence? What scale then was it he would lack either to demolish what was no longer relevant and essential or to discern and construct what was truly and clearly needed – even though no one saw it as yet?

If then the responsibility for all this still lay with him he would have to confess he had become a poor, an inefficient engineer: and he would know the necessity had now been born (the driver groaned with distaste) to feed himself and clothe himself upon eyes of mineral substitution, the artist's mask, the animal or plant of camouflage and vision. He would turn then, out of a curious despair, to someone or something he may have always unconsciously disregarded and despised, someone or something he would find himself driven now to *push* into the religious obscurity of moon or canal, the realm or depth of place he could not yet truly visualize for himself; someone who would appear surprisingly intact and whole, residual but unaffected by the landscape of fact, totally without – at that stage – the consciousness of having been actually set in motion or conscripted or wounded by another in the way the driver himself had once been free of such a dubious conviction.

And then – as if to illumine the dreamer's barricade of doubt – the dwarfed lamp of place shone like the grain of a skull: each hole of brightness which marked the ground delimited its own monstrous key of insertion and shadow like the blind solid glare of nature's fire, made tolerable to the inner camera of its reflective streaming eye within a phenomenal room of its own making, dark glasses against the sun; or like the conversion of the manufacturer's secret watermark upon an envelope held aloft against the flare of a match. So secret and inconstant the exit of image was, it concealed its dark issue in a new relation-ship of proportion out of disproportion.

And it was within these bars of secrecy that the framework of a parent scaffold reared its head and began to emerge again at last: the dreamer's twin obsession was clearer than ever now. And he (the driver) – stepson in vicarious stepfather, friend in vicarious brother – recoiled, on glimpsing this, as from his own growing surrender to the logic of unfamiliar truth... *It* was clothing him with the necessity of acknowledging the cloak of otherness, retirement into so little and obscurity of movement into so much: the conviction drove him – and had been driving him all along though he had never seen it – into a sphere of reduction and an arm of extensive feeling; the meeting ground of *two*, and he was indelibly associated with *one*.

Within it – within the globe of one and the indistinct preserves of the other – lay the key to an open consolidation the one could no longer support and carry; that one was standing ceaselessly upon the moving threshold of relinquishing it to the touch or residue of the other so that *it* (key and medium) could still exist in the grasp of one frail body of instinct as it unlocked the instant dust of another; in continual process of establishing a door for the one to issue through the other – through the logic of dreadful performance and execution into the principle of the ultimate breakdown of the wealth of injustice within the living witness of open fact.

It was both sliding rule and sliding scale of place with a reflex not merely of its own but of unpredictable room for transac-tion between TWO – one party to which was involved in the other's endless task of freedom (as the other was involved in the dazed circumvention of the ONE) of gauging and revising the dizzy scaffold of conceptions of the misconception – and misconceptions of the conception of revolving embrace, en-trance and exit.

7

It was a strange company – TWO and IT – though who *it* was no one could say: a crumbling scarecrow perhaps, the key to…? *It* possessed nevertheless a backbone and a single eye which turned and looked – without appearing to make any effort to see – both ways in the same blank crude instant: a blankness of question and expression which was as deceptive as a mirror made of headless stone or feature of glass made of heartless water. For this sculpture of blankness – in spite of its associa-tion with a nightmare hardness or an unstable dimension – was one of the curious ways of freedom, a live negative and unsleeping signal within the field of each past footfall and of every future captive formation: it was the embodied *currency* of lifelessness to repudiate the absolute reign or stillness of death. The medium of place (the scarecrow declared) had never died as was popularly depicted in the fictions of the day. And IT was engaged – even as it supported and bore the company of TWO – in preparing a new map of the fluid role of instinct, the ancient flight and landslide of which had never ceased continu-ing to move and outline an inherent traverse and cradle of regeneration in answer to the arrested dialogue of legend in the model despatches of love and prisons of hate, blind of Age and fold of Youth.

Item of Reconstruction: Diary recalling Fall into Ancient Passage – 20 years ago – Raven's Head. This Late Entry 30th July 1964: the Cat with Nine horned Lives painted on the Door of Present Book.

I was addressed by the walls of memory in a curious hallucinatory shorthand: STOP Equals LIGHTNING Exit. DON'T PANIC. Turn LEAVES of SUBTERRANEAN catalogue.

I framed a question in reply: was it possible to see at this stage – with emblematic eyes – or feel – with "dead" whiskers, cat – the end of the long tunnel out of blockage and catastrophe?

I can still perceive memory's chain of replies to my question like a long thundering train which still runs through this short timeless day – stranger and stranger snapshots still of those of us who recall the final – so it seemed – station of ourselves in time and space. And we (one obscure member of us, at any rate) may stumble therefore – in the end – who knows? – upon the flashing settlement and page of truth.

I confess quite openly that the picture and design of fact surrounding the crash (the crumbling reconnaissance car, plane, call it what you will, came down in the bush approximately north of Raven's Head) is – and always was from the beginning – architecturally unclear and unsound to me – unpredictable vacancy of ascent or block of descent? – and to everyone I have met to this day and hour who claim to have cleared or witnessed some such closed instantaneous event. And it is from within this stunned, breathless, postmortem (everyone believed this to be so for a long time) vision of recollection that a conception – or misconception – of the reality of the thing emerges after centuries, ages of haphazard penetration and shifting movement it seems. To speak of it as twenty calendrical years is to frame into shorthand all eternity with two curled strokes of a pen. Truth or absurdity?

I am grateful for one childlike endless obsession I entertained for a certain length and breadth of crushed time – poetic inversion as it may seem in the light of everything – which sticks out a mile to this day. Was it he who crept and crawled that last mile to save me or I to unlock him? I still like to think it was I who saved L——'s life, and not he mine, in the nick of time. Recurring balloon of dream or gauge of reality? For on that afternoon when I (it was on the tip of my tongue to say *he*) succeeded – more dead than alive – in finding a way through the jungle, nine months after I had been left for dead, I arrived in time to prove to the authorities I was a living soul and not the dead beast they swore they had seen.

L—— was released from the prison hospital (which was all that was standing between him and execution), the conviction against him quashed. The violent quarrel we had had over the woman Hebra the day before I was killed, so it was consistently reported, had weighed heavily against me (my mind still wanders in a trap); I should have said – against him: the time of trial. Whose neck was it, after all, his or mine in our eternal triangle, parent scaffold, step-parent, jealous room for lovers? It was the old sickening arch of half-comic ancestral half-light everyone approaches by way of mortal excuse and psychological riddling instinct.

It was not only the dark brush with Hebra our self-accusers built upon. The feud and myth of Sorrow Hill went deeper still and farther back. Anything to circumscribe their own fear of explosive nature in one and to relieve (or relive) their helplessness through another.

Presumably they reckoned he had flung me out of the window, miraculously judging the space and saving himself at the same time. He was their tigercat wizard and scapegoat, after all. And I, beyond a shadow of doubt, had confirmed this by springing up, at the last minute, alive. God knows who or what I was supposed to be at this juncture save that in their minds, and mine, an equation – destined to salvage a certain area of recollection – began to form – the sweep of nothing equals everything. Or to put it in a personal nutshell – the extinction or rekindling of one confirms a witness either way which equals two.

The CRASH – which I am now aware demolished not only their conventional presence but my fixed senses as well of room and absence from them – broke through to a passage of long-lost existence wherein the total deprivation of every clipped assumption of relative circumstance took ages to grow into the living fable of reality. The shepherd of the prowling bush and his grandson appeared out of nowhere. (Every attempt to locate them has been made since my recovery but the actual and original fierce and equally mild doctors of the masked ages are still not to be found.) How did I contrive – in the void of the mind which seems so long ago – to stitch a wild apprehension of them together? Glaring touch of conceit: fallacy. Needless to say it was they who obscurely measured and needled me when they found me lying on the ground. Rumpelstiltskin threads bristled like the wisest whiskers. A stitch in time saves nine. Cat's eyes fabric. Balloon skin pattern. Skyscraper tapestry. *The toy cow jumped over the toy moon.* I felt at a growing animal loss that they were refashioning me and escalating me into the flying sequence of a dwarf and the lofty imitation of a child.

THE FIRST BURIED IMAGES which returned to me (long before I actually saw the face of grandfather or grandson) were the womb and carriage of a dream I had forgotten. I saw myself moving away from myself within a dimension over which I appeared to have little control. I succeeded in returning to myself and to the consciousness of where I now stood on higher ground. My recollection of rearing up over myself – if I may so put it – actually arose in association with the feeling of a morsel in my mouth. I tried to spit it out but the cavity of teeth and tongue acquired an unsuspected pull and hold which made me swallow in spite of myself. I was situated, I discerned, not beneath but above the northern gateway of Raven's Head canal and I recalled – as I became aware of biting into the food in my mouth – how I had walked away helplessly and fearfully from myself only a moment ago, descended into the canal, crossed an ageless pit, and recrossed back to where now once again I stood.

Whoever I was, whom I now recalled, in startled intensity, and saw as if it were actually someone else in process of being drawn helpless and obscure, appeared to have moved on the spur of one moment to gain a shelter which stood, across from him, on the opposite side of the canal. The rain had suddenly started falling (this was his apparent reason and excuse) – long sad crystal lines of water which penetrated to one's skin. He swallowed, crossed the canal, bending almost double in order to crawl into the low shelter he gained on the other bank. The rain soon stopped and like a child on a rocking-horse – half-horse, half-rider – he retraced his steps across his grave of hallucination, without actually falling as he feared.

He had no notion how food or halter came back into his mouth – as if he had never actually moved from the same spot (or as if the very ground of sustenance may have moved itself unobtrusively forwards and back): in bewilderment and frustration he wanted to spit this stubborn root of sensation out but was forced to chew and swallow as if it were a living responsible guilty thing. He knew in this instant he would have to begin from the very obscure beginnings of everything to grapple with each form of strange support and community – moving apparently at open angles in an unbridled capacity of space or time but stunned by him or stunning him all the same into a new-born sense of the active density of riding context or overlapping station. FOOD AND SHELTER. It was the quickest rationalization he (or I?) indulged in like a blurred signpost or banner, leash as well as conception of ruling spirit of place.

Slowly he was becoming aware of the presence of persons saddled by things (and things saddled by persons) in a stunned world to which he now began to perceive he belonged: so stunned everything was that each action he witnessed, the performance of hand or instrument, possessed a strange "inside-out" inevitability belonging to levels as well as agents of a certain incalculable freedom from the ancient obsessions of life. He saw each one in this new revealing light of ridiculous bondage with the eye of one freshly woken though a curious shadow of restraint still lay upon him. The unsettling conviction was dawning within that they (he and the other) – however supremely conscious now of a past relationship – doer or done, server or served, runner or run – which they had forgotten and which they now dreamt to see in all entirety – might still be involved in a blind paradox and carriage (might still be involved in a tunnel of darkness surrounding their line of sight to match, even now, the radius of presence I remembered treading in cloaked awareness of myself or itself) which distanced us still within the most intimate moments of recall – one from the other – variable degrees of magnetic obscurity or areas of illusory contact. The drama of consciousness in which we were involved, part-knowing, part-unknowing, dim and voluntary, illuminating and involuntary, was infinite and concrete, simple and complex at the same time.

He was aware all at once that his feet were standing naked on the ground. And he began descending a staircase of land. Not into the middle of an absent river this time. Down steps instead which drew him into a small but unexpectedly ornate visionary room, the floor decorated with stable squares like a draughtsboard. The attendant within divided his attention – polishing the floor as well as shining one shoe which he held aloft in his hand. He was a salesman of parts it appeared: SHOES FOR SALE. His reaction on seeing his customer was consistent in its divided reflection, the trespass of apparent being in all community. The fact was – he was instantly obsessed, on seeing the other, with the notion of acquiring a sturdy fellow for the reluctant shoe he had mounted on one hand. A long boot, he cried, to go with the shoe. The customer was properly taken aback but flattered all the same by the request made of him to supply – out of a forgotten store of secrets – the missing boot the salesman needed as if it was not he (the customer), after all, who wanted to clothe himself but the inverse salesman (sophisticated beggar rather than crude middleman proprietor) whose advertised wish or will he was being called upon – in a game of elaborate moves – to erect and fulfil.

As they faced each other the infant dawn of ancient recollection strengthened: he (the customer) felt he had struck a bargain with the salesman in the shape of a beggar on old Water Street. Half-bandaged feet. Decrepit suit. One trouser leg rolled up, the other dangling down. The battered serge neither wet nor dry; and the customer was drawn by the spreading gravy of fabric. Was it his own blurred spirit of seasonal image? Yellow and black and green. The worn blood of autumn, black in winter, transparent in summer.

In my Father's house are many mansions.

Blood. The customer looked startled by the canvas of *blood*. How could this be? It was yellow still and black and green.

Were these then the legend of the bargain they struck as they played for time to present the map… transubstantiation… of blood? The black and gold dress of the green beggar advertised an enigmatic fluid salesman for one project of buried innocence: the innocent unborn "soul" who was destined to be charged with an account for murder. Better not to emerge and live. What a ludicrous collective design and open self-accusation this was. Megalomania and despair or the prison of overcoming the sacrificial need in – and of – humanity? But would not someone always be found – in the midst of the "dead" seal and ransom of everything – to subscribe – without even knowing how or why – to the "living" mutilation of the scarecrow? The answer of certain death and hate was void. That of the *quick* unconscious pageant of love an appointment with the meaningful Victim of all who served to blazon and rebuke, in his own born transcendental right, the meaningless power of lust in the Victor: he might be lifeless or stunned and footsore but he still arose in the nick of time… Save that it might still prove too late for all if Hebra, the vulgar muse or soul, had died – on the long buried road – of their epidemic disease, the victor's hand of strangling bodily lust, the victim's of *empty* strangled bodiless love. But how could the statuesque ghost of such painful arousal or conflict die? Hebra was equally a grotesque substitute – as repulsive as every appearance of conniving victim – for the timeless contradictory spouse they (victor and victim) both needed whether they were rich man or poor salesman, customer, artist or engineer. The art of a growing drunkard lay simply in each unthinking draught of the variegated blood of life, which made him the bloated twin of successive acts of compulsive mutilation on behalf of – was it a dream from beginning to end? – the pitiful and pitiless shrunken reality of freedom.

LETTER ADDRESSED TO LOCATION ENGINEER,
RAVEN'S HEAD

14th–15th August 1964

Dear L——,

I am now in a position to send you this partial witness of the confession I have been promising so long to make – *The Eye of the Scarecrow*.

Thank you very much indeed for the ancient photographs, clippings, old covenant, letters etc. etc. which you despatched to me c/o Night's Bridge Post Office.

Poor Scarecrow! it was his confession – he said he strangled her – which saved my neck. It is strange but at times I feel curiously drawn to him, then the horror of self-mutilation and self-extension – the image of conscience and consciousness – makes it seem both too evil and too good to be true. I remind myself that he may have possessed the blackest motive and to entertain a shred of affection for him – a self-confessed murderer – is the grimmest challenge to issue out of fixture and skeleton, cupboard of the past. I swear to myself – in order to rebuke every slight inclination to gratitude or love – that he did not come forward simply to stretch a helping hand to me: it was his "holy" pride which could not bear the thought of surrendering to the accursed cage of Hebra (she was the ugliest dead soul and mistress in the world one may ever hope to see); no flight was too much for him and the thought that I – project and twin in his bow of creation – should suffer punishment and death in his astronomical mission and deed would have shattered all upright carriage and future hope in him. It is the contemplation of such an instrument of jealous time, *which I am at a loss to know how to bend or bear* – it is so resolute and strong – that sobers me in the end to view him once again in a new and unashamed gentle light. Yes, I confess it, after all these years, a true conception of depth and affection.

His confession it is which frees us now to make ours – if we wish. For – it is the plain arrow of truth – if he had not come forward when he did, we would have remained locked in the inertia of our time; you would have died with the uncertain conviction whether I really knew you to be innocent or guilty (in fact it would not now matter) and I in turn would have gone to my inevitable target or scaffold or end equally unknowing what you had drawn in truth out of me.

It is likely that you would have breathed not a murmur of protest and would have blamed yourself for everything. Old stoic! But I would have reacted differently. Self-mockery. Shock. How could one live to escape – as we had so often done – the string of disaster, fire and flood, to face the bar of crude unjust anticlimax? Why, our reconnaissance machine had crashed. Remember? But flung us out with a sudden snap into a jungle of miraculous survival. And still…

As it was, the shock of "ultimate" liberation was the most cunning and desperate blow of all when it came. For when Scarecrow came forward – pork-knocking beggar that he was – and swore he loved the devil of a woman – I was lost in the obsession that this was our nightmare soul and trick – something you had successfully engineered (and I dreamt I performed) to give us more time to manufacture a defence and case.

And so – God forgive me – the circumstances of deception seemed so brutally open and clear – I began to identify myself with *him* and with *you* (as if there stood over me every daring midwife and extension of folly): the strongest most unbearable pregnant blinding light of misunderstanding and understanding. I began (now I see it dimly and admit it) to read the unreflecting volume which the nature of everything – both timeless and absurd – was seeking to discharge and dismantle.

And even so I am still confused by time, the truly suffering elements of pitiless direction and miraculous chance: whose and what true universal innocence – the innocence of the One we share – do these ceaselessly appoint and confirm? I do not know if Scarecrow is not still a dark invention and excuse I presented to myself and *you* were the living undistorted representative one (untimely as all time is and therefore pitiful) who paid the ugliest and dearest prospective price for me…

It is this *consciousness* of the continuous erosion of self-made fortifications that is the "material" of my Confession – which you, out of some inexplicable motive and curious humour, declare yourself in need of at this time in spite of all your resources of ageless simplicity. But then you were always waiting at the door of self-exile and within the flesh of stone, without appearing to mind over much the tragic self-sufficiency and failure and meaninglessness of invented modes and self-created things…

May God forgive me for what insensitive and insensible fury I believe I saw and what sensitive and sensible glory I still do not appear to make or *see*.

IDIOT NAMELESS

8

HIS OWN ACTION sprang out of the long unconscious habit of trying to fashion her into his own image against the fear of surprising alien beauty or ugliness in a passive state of nature.

How to make her feel in the end – his hand moved from thigh to throat – what she had never suffered before – his sense of self-construction, likeness to humiliation? He had always assumed until now that it was admirable for her to be the senseless humiliated one, proper model or contemptible subject, tenant of his whim of erection, unthinking whore. This charmed circle served to give him an ascendancy over her – his principal commodity: mud and fleshpot of dreams. She was his to rule, chop, barter. To do with – on occasions – as he liked. But with each deadening stranglehold – something he had never quite bargained for in the beginning happened – the price of execution rose by leaps and bounds: the sliced features of "living" death withdrew into something as simple, direct, economic as that. It dawned on him – in a way he had never reckoned before – that she was every man's meat, the technically rich and the technically poor, and he was now being called upon to spend more and still more upon her.

IT (the transaction of indignity) had never presented itself in this harsh motive light before, the light of an incongruous initiative she possessed which was capable of overpowering him rather than being overpowered by him. It was he who was becoming the subject of her encirclement. The shock of this robbed him immediately of all feeling of arbitrary possession: and the numb consequence, wood, stone, clod of earth, grew into a new senseless demand. Like someone and something so taken by surprise in the marketplace of habit, HE and IT began to dislodge themselves from an old, undeviating chain of deadly circumstance. *It* became not only a high-priced tag but a priceless jewel whose rarity bred every astonished witness of jealousy or love. And he was the most afflicted witness whose need of one model and ideal economic servant transcended the DREAMING ANCIENT link of service and demand. This magnetic dawn – age of decomposition and recomposition – drew him to make her over beyond all mere plastic lines of facile purchase or ignorant necessity into something he felt he now desired her to uphold and see. His true submissive horn of likeness. Engine of humiliation. Love.

That he had run her down and destroyed his image in the process was a possibility he never dreamt extended beyond the impotency of himself, the impotency of all men who grow from infancy into the ancient riddle of a premature acceptance of weakness, born and reborn burrowing instinct, the nebulous current of the dynamo...

A transparent vehicle of age and youth he was (and she was no longer a mere crushed bone of contention), an enterprise set in incredible proportion and relation – CAPACITY and DENSITY: the capacity of unique digestion, consciousness; the density of friction between space and thing, flight and ground, making the sparks of instinct fly.

It was in this intoxicated "blind" tradition and unflinching, involuntary strength (in which he deprived her of every soft catlike option she had once been at liberty to exercise) that he killed her; and then – perceiving a glimmer of the full light of indefatigable living currency, apparent horror, integral reason and melting unreason he had unwittingly invoked – he gave himself up to be sold to the highest bidder, sensing the death of "economic" love and "ideal" opportunity but the likelihood of enduring recompense in a "soul" of liberty. And thus became truly himself a hideous engine of reality in the empirical eye of Justice, standing on the baffling scaffold of classical conversion and compassion – a new age of self-confession and self-proportion.

He had killed her in order to possess her within new limits (the ultimate cancellation of greed?) – digestion and capacity: at the jealous INN OF THE QUARTERING OF THE COW where she had taken her last promiscuous rich lover like a morsel in her own right. This was final as a blow of stone, the natural and unnatural battleground of the harsh senses and sexes. And yet he was still incredulous – how could he really have engineered such an impossible breathless stroke? He clung to both grain and hand of incredulity, "future" enlightenment, constitution, innocent understanding, like a Child in a womb of ancestral fantasy whose every unborn move is a refusal to bow to an inventory of mechanical fates and imprints.

Two months – even less – remained to him, and these would embrace nine in all of rude trial and conception: the Scarecrow (with which I had invested myself as if I were now intent on breaking through from within) accepted the sentence of death passed on him.

He sat in his cell-like parent sculpture, pregnant witness; the feminine clay of his hands moved the pawns on a draughtsboard: each piece in his fingers curiously alive, scraped clean as the dust of memory from the sole of his boot. Sometimes the game of conscience he played was blank as an empty slate, sometimes haunted by the subversive cloak of identity within, the meaning of each day's uplifted word towards the crown of silence.

For if indeed his jealous claim to the art of murder remained unflinching and still sensitive to truth, might he not have succeeded beyond his wildest dreams in supporting and recreating the enigma of life – the twins of breath and breathlessness, animus and anima? Future instinct of the borderline. To be or not to be. In reality – how could there be in this respect any true choice since the alternatives were invested with groundless self-sufficiency? In fact they were not so invested and never had been. THE GHOST AND HAMLET. Both were the apprehensive soul or image of an unknown capacity – death the image of unreflecting life or life the soul of unreflective death: the scales of being were still melting beyond or within each other, infinitely perhaps treacherously closed or infinitely perhaps fearfully open.

The art of murder. In this lay the supreme paradox: the surprising and surprised lifeblood within each invented (or inverted) pawn or thing. No man's land of living achievement.

Oh to be born without the stain of death. Could it be that he was slowly going mad or inexorably and miraculously sane? He knew the child which would bear his name (most curious spirit-child of an absent parent-to-be) was expected within a couple of months. Perhaps – who could tell – within the hour of execution, *his* execution. He wanted to laugh but his lips were drawn; stiff. No wonder it became necessary, in statuesque advance, to paint, erect – invest himself with – the overriding garment of two concerted women until wife-and-mother confessed to the feature of solipsis, ageless mistress, appetite, Hebra: and Hebra herself changed and acquired the soul and expression of patented youth. Was this a self-critical and incalculable conversion... art... transubstantiation... of eloquent blood?

The shadow of a hidden self was his, the function of "myself" in the limbo of himself – would such an instinctive and subjective spirit-child (weaned on the disasters of the ages) consent, in turn, to be hollowed and thereby apparently inflated into an unconventional and illuminating room of endless, treacherous, growing proportions – the bed and skull and crossbones of self-discovery and self-parody, rich man, poor man, beggarman, king? He cried to me and to the skeleton proprietors of love: and with each move on his canvas and board of earth sought to lay bare each swollen, still shrunken square of flesh – an incredible design of bleeding, wounded affections which in another light appeared bloodless ingrained lines of living hardship rather than lifeless sensibility, any extension or part of which might serve – in a moment of bewildering stricken reality – to enclose or equally strip and dismantle one's preconception of guilt.

It was as if indeed I sat facing him in the dense and transparent cell of his movable, immovable, deceptive prison and person: as if I had arrived in this backward, unexpected pregnant way to the goal of my long quest. Paradoxical womb: cloak: long lost father and new-found son. Distorted mother and distorting generation. A host of terrible questions arose I needed time to ask and place in mute perspective.

I was drawn to the windows, CORPUSCLES OF SUN, glowing intermittently: the mansions of blood, illusion and reality. In one framed picture or neighbouring room the walls were almost black. The colour of smoke. A figure moved within shadow and stone: fished on his hands and knees for a flake of soap which had slipped from him and was skidding across the floor. He recovered it; resumed washing his hands: basin... room... for the grease of lust to cleanse the mud of love.

It was this shocking awareness of mutual involvement and obsession which woke him all at once and he saw himself within his own flowing and unwavering reflection of shadow. For within the basin of truth he was related to an unbending scrubbed companion, one who had never yielded pride of place to the other until he saw himself how black and fluid it was. And though he was looking into what seemed the next room, under his nose, as it were, the distance between himself and itself was enormous, light years, water years, blood years, the years of fire and smoke; still the very enormity of intimate contact made it impossible for him to dislodge the tie of agelessness, the sense of being tied to an age of agelessness: if one appeared to stand nodding but still the other refracted and moved, and when one appeared to run and sleep the other kept a dark pace, too, and woke, moving as before and yet still, so that the specific weight and gravity of the distant colour of consciousness within and without one's pool rested upon each crumb of the self-same purification and self-recognition.

Each line, elevation, window, room – within the mansion – that he was still able to perceive from his broad vantage point – was raised to a kind of inverse mathematical power of spirit, the indissoluble link of space, relief from density, conscious-ness of unconsciousness. As a result he was quick to jump to his own arbitrary conclusion: a greedy – if not bloodthirsty capacity – was on the fringe of baring itself to him, which would support the privilege of beholding the endless procession of the ages, eternally and perfectly unaware of itself – within or without which – crowd scenes or bedroom scenes – he himself would therefore remain logically unremembered and unseen.

But – he caught his breath sharply – the thought had barely touched his lips like a seductive kiss, it seemed, when he felt a stifling burden and sensation of remorse, horror, stupefaction. Not that he dreaded the insubstantial jealous touch of a mere hand, heart, throat, elusive knife or blunt rope. These were, after all, transient signals, however cruel, of dimension and form leading to repose, the liberal form of death. It was the sheer limitless *contraction* he was experiencing which he now dreaded and which he had summoned all unreflecting upon himself: the heightened power of devouring hope or senseless despair to visualize a timeless ultimatum, iota of breath, infinite or infinitesimal scale: conquest of the minutest square root, *space he could not at present dream to bear.*

The fixed walls appeared to be closing in upon him inch by wall, wall by foot, and out of this arose the stifling grain of uncertainty; a trick of light falling like painted rain: rain or brush of elements sweeping over him and affecting – so it seemed – all space around him which was gradually filling and disappearing (without however emptying him, even as it threatened to obliterate him, of or from the solid dust of canvas).

It was an instinct for well-nigh unendurable contraction he had invoked and the sense of impending breathlessness began to fuse its own *breath* – mist – upon the plane surfaces of his life. In fact the image of womb as well as room was falling flat in the end as though once seen from its overwhelmed and his overwhelming angle it ceased to exist as a void. Indeed every conventional distinction between volume and surface became inextricably close and unreal.

For since a cube is subject to filling or hollowing, it subsists in potential depletion or repletion of itself (its own paradox of vain expansion): but since the thinnest film or surface into which it may ultimately resolve is susceptible to an abstract measurement in depth still, however unimaginably frail and indistinct, THIS *(and no other) lives in a true body of density which demolishes at one stroke the technical, subjective hollow or void; but remains, as it were, technically full still, a dripping mist or sweat of proportion, incapable* NOW *of being dug into or dug out, inner space (its true unassailable possession), indestructible, faint scale or measure of One universe.*

It was as if he had had his first major object lesson in spite of everything: cargo of relief: sail of consciousness. Which sought to lift from him (in a fleeting but far-reaching incalculable design) the pregnant despair of the "born" dead. Such a carriage of misconception, wheel of toppling curiosity, dread, faded into vessels it lay within him now to translate and carry like the potent irony of dust, tenants of soul whose disposition he would begin to store and build, seal of ancient hope, spiked cannon of sunrise and sunset, secret faces of sky and earth. And at the end or beginning of each light obsessed cloud, roadway of day and night, they would arise like members of his own uncertain fastness of life to shoot their instinctive ultimatum of sun at each sinister – so it seemed – barred gateway he had himself made: rainbow, condensation, constellation to enlighten him in place of the ambivalent guard or parent of old he still half-remembered he wished to question within this new almost blank goal of a past presence or present.

Was it that he had truly forgotten half of a "lived" future, the assured dictation of the future from which he had retreated into the sentence of the womb in the way the servants and tenants of nature – mask of earth, seed, sun – were continuously striking and retiring, aiming and crumbling within the self-creation of each last burning fateful arrow?

THE DAWN OF FREEDOM. The dusty answer flashed through and through hollow artist and prisoner like grains of an unproven, even unprovable manifesto...

9

MANIFESTO OF THE UNBORN STATE OF EXILE
NIGHT'S BRIDGE

Dear L——,

Language is one's medium of the vision of consciousness. There are other ways – shall I say – of arousing this vision. But language alone can express (in a way which goes beyond any physical or vocal attempt) the sheer – the ultimate "silent" and "immaterial" complexity of arousal. Whatever sympathy one may feel for a concrete poetry – where physical objects are used and adopted – the fact remains (in my estimation) that the original grain or grains of language cannot be trapped or proven. It is the sheer mystery – the impossibility of trapping its own grain – on which poetry lives and thrives. And this is the stuff of one's essential understanding of the reality of the original Word, the Well of Silence. Which is concerned with a genuine sourcelessness, a fluid logic of image. So that any genuine act of possession by one's inner eye is a subtle dispersal of illusory fact, dispossession of one's outer or physical eye.

The stillness of consciousness (which stillness is always penetrating itself in its own activity) is not the contrived or self-created stillness of a property of the physical world. In the same way the trespass of consciousness is not the same movement one consumes with a physical immediacy, apprehension, sense. This subtle logic of image and transformation in consciousness of all one's apparent and stable and persuasive functions is the meaning of language. For language because of its untrappable source transforms – in a terrifying well-nigh unendurable perspective – every subjective block and fixture of capacity. *In my Father's house are many mansions.*

The ideal of a concrete poetry (it would be sounder I feel to say granular poetry) is an instinctive recognition of the mysterious architecture and spirit of place in the far-reaching capacity of consciousness. But to attempt to pin the grains down is to prolong the agony of misunderstanding the nature of language itself.

Of course behind this attempt – the pathetic language of "dead" things – lies a motive concealed from those who are involved in their purposeless game. It is an unconscious attempt to break down the indigestible disease of subjective fashion – to find in nature an innocent array of objects and the ground, as well, of classical unity free from a vested interest in arbitrary mood or colour. But right here a subtle misconception arises in the apparent concretization of the word "ground" which once seen in consciousness belongs to an ageless flight of "instinct".

Let this hidden motive or buried conviction appear to be *seen* (something quite different to what one sees physically on the ground) and the vision clamours for its true word of expression. So much so that it can become an appalling deaf-and-dumb show (or quest) for the wholeness of spiritual recognition and responsibility throughout every crook and cranny of things: a show which seeks unhappily to break the doom of perpetuating a "ground" of error – hereditary misconception – fixed instinct – misrepresentation starting with the very apparent birth of a "future" language of possibilities. This abortive classical grain or ground needs to suffer a truer return to the womb of subjection, subjective error and will, to see its own capacity for change which lies still and unpredictably beyond the self-evident decline of every "murdered" or "murderous" foundation. The continuous birth of poetry needs to be more (and less in its true cryptic outcry and dialectical landslide) than an imitation of a preservative fluid: it is the lifeblood of *seeing* and responding without succumbing – in the very transparent mobility of consciousness – to what is apparently seen and heard.

As such it subsists on its own apparent losses as nothing else can, provided that the instincts of fluid image – inseparable from the visionary truth of nature – are indeed their own untranslatable rebuff, barrier or privilege.

Beyond this lies the original well of silence, that "silence" which language alone can evoke, a depthlessness of sound heard and digested in the bloodstream of the mind which is the closest one can come to entering the reality of the living circulation of the "dead".

I find myself laying bare what is perhaps the most secret conviction I jealously hold – I was so deeply moved by your generous acknowledgment of my Confession which you accepted, in some curious overlapping way, as if it had sprung from your own need as well. I was moved because I knew you would never have implied this if I had not – in the first place – surrendered (or tried to surrender) every obscure and thoughtless and perhaps *cunning* gesture of will exercised by me in the past – the greedy will to action and to blanket all reaction.

In the premises of open surrender lie the equality of touch and conviction I have always inwardly desired and we both now sense and realize as never before: the true beginnings of possible dialogue, the breath of all unobstructive physicality one receives standing upon a borderline (as silent words stand on their speaking page) between an Imagination capable of reconciling unequal forms present and past and an Imagination empty of self-determined forms to come, blank frames, indwelling non-resemblance, freedom from past, present, future form and formlessness. *It is in this unpredictable and paradoxical light one begins to forgive and be forgiven all.*

And I have much of whom and of which to ask reconciliation in the present and forgiveness in the future.

I would not have dreamt of such a possibility in the far-off days we knew without feeling either instantly ashamed of the sentiment or instantly hard-hearted: arteries of willpower: should I impose reconciliation and forgiveness on others or accept the imposition of forgiveness and reconciliation from others? Neither questionable alternative is what I now mean...

The key to my present meaning lies in a crumbling of the will which may be seen in another sense as the breakdown of a series of tyrannous conception or misconception – the cruel strength of individual legacy. I feel this position (from your point of view as well as mine) is clearer than ever now. For there are many approaches to this I appear to possess which seem to me indistinguishable, in certain respects, from your own excavations or penetrations of Raven's Head. I am not suggesting that I could ever bear the continuous burden you do – unflagging concentration and the confrontation of models of anguish. (I am thinking in particular now of the brutal snapshots of Raven's Head you sent to me which I shall soon discuss with you in my own light.) I know you will instantly turn away from the label "anguish". Why must one dwell upon or relapse into anguish of recollection you will say – except in the most relative illusory concrete terms – when confronted by an endless task which frees one from stages of subjection and subjectivity, and points towards a classical revelation of withdrawal or momentum in every part of a "living" universe?

Let it all rest in my weak part then – each confession of stifling bitterness which seems at times to settle again and lift, only with the greatest difficulty, above myself. This solitary uncreative admission remains purely individual, purely mine. As though I am capable of becoming conscious of being the rich "dead" self-sufficient, self-explanatory thing, after all, while everything else around me – despised and poor – appears to grow into a universal meaningless secret, deserving once again of contempt, because of an inward and meaningful retrenchment and participation – a brooding capacity – I fear to confess I must suffer deeply with to understand – for a new unspectacular conception of life. Which reflects something else equally subjective and paradoxical and fearful too. It was I who pushed you into your present enterprise but I am glad I do not have your classical responsibilities to bear. They frighten me to death. And for this reason I would not know how to be envious of you, whatever the ultimate "glorious" self-sacrifice and apparent reward.

Nevertheless to return to what I said a moment ago. There are certain approaches to my *crumbling of the will* which are indistinguishable – in a remote and subjective form – from your own native and professional excavations and penetrations. It is as if sometimes (I hope you will forgive me) I have an involuntary but acute awareness of changing places with you. And for a fraction of an instant I am filled with a terrible dread of place and of standing irrevocably in your shoes. I know of no more frightful tyranny of misunderstanding. Misunderstanding of what? Misunderstanding of whom? Misunderstanding of where? It is the third unknown factor and question which brings the first bewildering faint landslide of relief. *And I am able to resume, as it were, the "potential" ground of self-exile, the unborn state of the world.*

Now in connection with the latest snapshots of Raven's Head: they shook me more than I can easily say. Made me ask myself: where was it and when was it that I was invalided out of Raven's Head? I would have given much to have been able to remain with the expedition (and yet as I said before I shudder at the thought of such concentration and responsibility) and to have crossed the ancient river with you and arrived at the ruined targets your pictures disclose. I was invalided out after the CRASH. But surely you must see, my dear L——, how bewildered I still am: what was – or is – this crash one speaks of, so inconclusively, that altered nevertheless decisively our twin misconception and conception of every flamboyant possessive thing? Sexual bolt of childhood or manhood? Frantic Bull's Eye of America or Europe? Globe of fantasy – Asia or Africa? Lost chart of remembrance or new-found continent? Blindfold of Day or Night's Bridge? Way of the Ancients or Ring of the Moderns? One can go on and on firing at the shadowy long tail of memory... The truth is – *I can't remember*. Evolution. Revolution. Regeneration. Collapse. All I can honestly say is that the potential fragments of recollection before and after GOD KNOWS WHAT are *alive* in a way I never suspected before.

Indeed it is here that you and I began, or still begin, to approach a meaningful conjunction and parting of the ways – essential way of "compulsive" withdrawal and incalculable way of "new" community. And yet *is it true* that I (within the person of obscurity) have really begun at last to know at the closest inviolable "negative" quarters the "flash" of explosive freedom you (within your globe or world) possess? The fear of such "exposure" arises nevertheless (even as one begins to dwell significantly in it) within premises of "privilege", bulb or state, attraction or repulsion, so that one may sometimes even discern one's individual longing and blindness in every snapshot of practical judgment (or misjudgment), absorption, calculating malice and self-indulgence: one may even discern one's fear of the capacity of another. And one may be driven as a consequence to erect one's sovereign of wish-fulfilment – as if it were the highest defence, vulgar accomplishment, presumptive darkness or light over and against the true ligament of person and thing. Which is to succumb ultimately to self-hatred or self-flattery, creed of miseducation, misrepresentation and folly...

The explosive question however remains inextricably woven within each "flash", living distinctive otherness, mysterious response or lack of response. The education of freedom – (and you have been one of my unconscious tutors in whom and with whom I grew into the heart of "negative" identity, self-contradiction, even "positive" loathing of the "ground" of "spirit") – begins with a confession of the need to lose the base concretion men seek to impose when they talk of one's "native" land (or another's) as if it were fixed and anchored in place. In this age and time, one's native land (and the other's) is always *crumbling*: crumbling within a capacity of vision which rediscovers the process to be not foul and destructive but actually the constructive secret of all creation wherever one happens to be. It is in the light of wisdom or compassion – across the divide of the ages perhaps – that one looks back and accuses (as well as excuses) oneself for succumbing again and again to that individual picture of self-imposed restriction and longing which arises, and which constitutes nostalgia for what is not and the anguish of helplessness in the face of what is: the ever-recurring posture of abortive sensibility which assists one (but only at some later less self-indulgent stage – fresh insight into living detail) to sympathize with the derangement of all creatures within history and circumstance who wander the face of the earth as if they were the "living" unfulfilled part of oneself and one were the "dead" fulfilled expression of their self...

Such a "graphic" inversion of privilege is the crumbling role of time in space and of one's pride and anguish. Which brings *me* face to face once again with the snapshot of your "black" cell in Raven's Head as if in one illuminating moment you and I were free of each other and yet apparently the same. And yet *you* – I cannot help feeling within the "pregnant" distance which enfolds us – must see it factually, even simply, in your explosive and elemental and indestructible right since it is I who must still confess, with a shameful start, to an ancient predisposition I have not yet shaken off, traces of lingering judgment and illness, the subjective emotion of being born into the inescapable conformity and finality of everything however liberating and far-reaching the actual kinship of event.

And indeed even now the "still" dread of change (that ancient "model" of freedom to change) still appears... catastrophic... nostalgic... I pored over the "black" portrait... forgot everything... remembered... What? Where? Was this the room of alien judgment... CONQUEST... into which we appeared to drop? THE ROOM OF THE FALL? Do I dream now for one choked instant as I stare into it – the figment of it – (half-comprehending, half-incomprehending nodding impractical joke) that you died there on the scaffold – distant night breathing within Raven's

Head – whilst I lived and fell and gasped, hand over hand of rope, until my feet touched the floor?

The walls were black. Cloud or smoke. The Ancient of Nights. You flashed your "dead" thought like the beam of a torch towards constellation, sky or roof. Someone had died for us, you said. THE UNINITIATE. ACCEPTANCE OF BLIND MURDER. Your voice was tranquil, cold and calm. Without a trace of my fierce hunger and dread and emotion for the premature rite of ancient meaning, governing intellect and clinical understanding. Was it you who had turned the arts and tables of science and dissection on me, after all, or I on you as before? I felt my face begin to crack in the light of your clear untroubled countenance.

The meaty limbs you drew to my attention (suspended from the roof) were peeled, raw, elongated vestiges of marble. That was all. *The Inn of the Quartering of the Cow*. The name rang a bell. It was as if I stood at the door of every skeleton, lightning cupboard, curiosity shop down the secret ladder of the ages. Skyscraper dinner, menu of… catastrophe (or ultimate salvation and universal digestion)? Generations past and generations to come.

All reflecting the long-suffering mate or animal one saw and still slew in the mind and strove to eat or devour once and for all: the brutal art of arts – the conquest of all consuming love and jealousy which made one quick to magnify the subject of lust or anguish on every self-sufficient occasion or in every self-sufficient apparition. Until one *saw* again the sheer "negative" burden of liberation within the positive rule or maw of the senses: liberation from "divine" stomach, from premature identity of self-torture rather than self-conquest, from greed, frustration, overfed memory, vicarious desire, mechanical rape, area of preservation and prediction. On the marbles of memory (the flesh of the past) and prediction (the flesh of the future) flashed and rose the inimitable "snapshot" of spirit upon the medium of helpless and backward self-sacrificial subject… And the dream of black inner space turned into new classical blood, dispossession of the straitjacket of time. *Memory and prediction: what then could these mean?* It was as if the celebrated torch in your hand blew out and nothing remained but to grope in the uncanny realm of forgotten portrait and room.

THE BLACK ROOMS

The room of the VISIONARY COMPANY

One pause of sunset, in particular, I recall now, like a station of feathered branches, half-tree, half-bird, lingering a long while in the sky before a train of frozen fire part-extinguished, part-melted itself into the ground. In the fulfilled poise of this moment, like a barrier of absorption between day and night, the reluctant smoke of sky and carriage of earth were drawn into singular consciousness of each other…

If I were to attempt to confine or draw an exact relationship or absolute portrait of what everything was before the stroke fell and created a void in conventional memory, I would have succumbed to the dead tide of self-indulgent realism. On the other hand, to travel with the flood of animated wreckage that followed after, is a different matter, a trusting matter in which I am involved – a confession that nothing immaterial and actual and eternal may have changed in the outlines of the past; and therefore since the nucleus of phenomenal catastrophe one envisages at any particular moment is just as likely as anything else to be an illusion, it is useless to believe one was, or is, ever possessed by articles of spirit without faith.

…the starkest bier of grave memory I knew, when as a boy on my way to school I sometimes encountered the "poor man's hearse" rolling towards me, painted black as shining coal.

113

...fearfully and inevitably... the explosive train of memory rolls along (mingling economic and political, metaphysical and dialectical physicians like an ancestral gathering of nurses...) *I dreamt I was standing alone in a large room...*

...THE STRIKING INNERMOST CHEMISTRY OF LOVE...

...from that moment my pagan scaffold, my visionary sport in nature, began crumbling secretly beyond the limits of the purity of obsession... And yet little though I knew it this was to prove a lifetime's poetry of science and a stubborn terrifying task.

...the melted scaffolding of all the years...

The Room of GENESIS

But now the very joylessness with which it had been constructed struck me like a curious revelation of mystical sorrow. I felt cold and strange, a religious stranger to all previous knowledge of emotion; and *emotion* – in such a void or context – became new, liberating, oblique, powerless to arouse an expenditure of energy to create the harm I saw I had already inflicted.

The sound of the clock was at first distant and somnolent but on gaining one's attentive reflection it developed into something as insistent as everything I had called upon to be made which groaned and protested. *The Night of self-initiation*, self-kinship, grew into celestial furniture, the great hearse rolled on, stitched planks held by the scissors of the universe, divisions of cloud within which glimmered the operations of space...

So it was I jumped forward into an echoing future (which is now with the dead voices of the past) and into a middle of a year –

a great procession – the striking year of every man's familiar obsession (1948 or 2048?)... the "timeless" footprints of a self-created self...

...*substitute*...

POSTSCRIPT OF FAITH IN DARK ROOM OF IDENTITY

My dear L——,
What obsessive validity your snapshots appear to have. I have been running through them again, grain and thread from the ghost of my beginning to the spirit of my end. Two things are as obsessional as they are clear. Freak of identity or law of reality?

One – Raven's Head is constructed out of curious subjective shapes indistinguishable at times from their environment, paper, wood and stone.

Two – this subjectivity in the material is a barrier and a challenge at all times within premises of universal life whose timeless currency and continuity have nothing to do with the pseudo-objective facets and factors of subjection and stability as such which may appear (depending on one's closed stand-point) admirably "good", "successful", "pleasing" or hideously "bad", "repellent", "confusing".

The approach then to the "classical" Raven's Head – the Raven's Head into which we are still to be born like creatures who may learn to dwell in a state of penetrative relationship and self-exile – cries out for two admissions.

One – a confession or admission of humility, the limited standpoint of the active and involved human person.

Two – (in order that *One* does not become a form of nihilism, the devil's lightning and creed) – a confession or admission of the mystery of capacity, the illumination of

115

capacity within which arises both the issue and sculpture of science, interior unpredictable dialogue, discharge of grace.

Two is of the greatest relative importance since IT confirms the "shut-in" person as both potential cornerstone and dimension (the "open" city) by confessing to a continuous and miraculous conception of "living" and "dead" nature, rehabilitation of the lost One, the unrealized One, the inarticulate One.

And this miraculous conception is timeless: since "timelessness" alone is capable of that, inflation and deflation of consciousness to sift and endure every subjective "contamination" and "ground": the quest of phenomenal space rather than phenomenal time. Inevitability of direction – implicit in the iron logic of time – crumbles, the legacy of time, false or unreliable memory, false or unreliable prediction. And the "distance" between objects of assessment and reassessment – the burden of individual guilt and collective history – appears like a participation of inviolable soul or presence within and above shattering confrontation, instinctive meeting as well as conjunctive parting beyond the senseless incline or decline of chronological age, the drought of will. In the end the weakest trickle of prayer can become one's treasure of fulfilment through no virtue in the aridity of the living (such as myself) save that One (such as you) endures beyond all fluid reckoning to provide an illuminating scale and measure of self-abandonment and self-recognition. THE WELL OF SILENCE. AMEN. Amen.

IDIOT NAMELESS
25th September 1964

116

Wilson Harris was born in New Amsterdam in British Guiana, with a background which embraces African, European and Amerindian ancestry. He attended Queen's College between 1934-1939, thereafter studying land surveying and beginning work as a government surveyor in 1942, rising to senior surveyor in 1955. In this period Harris became intimately acquainted with the Guyanese interior and the Amerindian presence. Between 1945-1961, Harris was a regular contributor of stories, poems and essays to *Kyk-over-Al* and part of a group of Guyanese intellectuals that included Martin Carter, Sidney Singh and Ivan Van Sertima. His first publication was a chapbook of poems, *Fetish*, (1951) under the pseudonym Kona Waruk, followed by the more substantial *Eternity to Season* (1954) which announced Harris's commitment to a cross-cultural vision in the arts, linking the Homeric to the Guyanese. Harris's first published novel was *Palace of the Peacock* (1960), followed by a further 23 novels with *The Ghost of Memory* (2006) as the most recent. His novels comprise a singular, challenging and uniquely individual vision of the possibilities of spiritual and cultural transcendance out of the fixed empiricism and cultural boundedness that Harris argues has been the dominant Caribbean and Western modes of thought.

Harris has written some of the most suggestive Caribbean criticism in *Tradition the Writer and Society* (1967), *Explorations* (1981) and the *Womb of Space* (1983), commenting on his own work, the limitations of the dominant naturalistic mode of Caribbean fiction, and the work of writers he admires such as Herman Melville.

Following the breakdown of his first marriage, Harris left Guyana for the UK in 1959. He married the Scottish writer Margaret Burns and settled in Chelmsford. Thereafter, until his retirement, Wilson Harris was much in demand as visiting professor and writer in residence at many leading universities.

ALSO BY WILSON HARRIS IN THE CLASSICS SERIES

Wilson Harris
Heartland
Introduction: Michael Mitchell
ISBN: 9781845230968; pp. 188; 2009; £7.99

Zechariah Stevenson, son of a wealthy businessman, is the watchman at a timber grant deep in the Guyanese interior. In flight from the scandal of a fraud and the connected disappearance of his mistress, Stevenson isolates himself in the forest, which he discovers is disturbingly alive and conscious. In this vulnerable state old certainties crumble. But he is guided by three ghostly revenants from Harris's previous novels: Kaiser who has become the storekeeper of the heartland; Petra a pregnant Amerindian woman and Da Silva, the pork-knocker, whose second death points Stevenson in the direction of a journey that crosses the boundaries between life and death. Harris, who was for many years a surveyor in the Guyanese hinterland, creates a powerfully physical sense of the complex relationship between the human and the natural worlds.

CARIBBEAN MODERN CLASSICS NOW AVAILABLE

Jan R. Carew
Black Midas
Introduction: Kwame Dawes
ISBN: 9781845230951; pp. 272; May 2009; £8.99

This is the bawdy, Eldoradean epic of the legendary 'Ocean Shark' who makes and loses fortunes as a pork-knocker in the gold and diamond fields of Guyana, discovering that there are sharks with far sharper teeth in the city. *Black Midas* was first published in 1958.

Jan R. Carew
The Wild Coast
Introduction: Jeremy Poynting
ISBN: 9781845231101; pp. 240; May 2009; £8.99

First published in 1958, this is the coming-of-age story of a sickly city child, sent away to the remote Berbice village of Tarlogie. Here he must find himself, make sense of Guyana's diverse cultural inheritances and come to terms with a wild nature disturbingly red in tooth and claw.

Neville Dawes
The Last Enchantment
Introduction: Kwame Dawes
ISBN: 9781845231170; pp. 332; April 2009; £9.99

This penetrating and often satirical exploration of the search for self in a world divided by colour and class is set in the context of the radical hopes of Jamaican nationalist politics in the early 1950s. First published in 1960, the novel asks many pertinent questions about the Jamaica of today.

Edgar Mittelholzer
Corentyne Thunder
Introduction: Juanita Cox
ISBN: 9781845231118; pp. 242; April 2009; £8.99

This pioneering work of West Indian fiction, first published in 1941, is not merely an acute portrayal of the rural Indo-Guyanese world, but a work of literary ambition that creates a symphonic relationship between its characters and the vast openness of the Corentyne coast.

Andrew Salkey
Escape to an Autumn Pavement
Introduction: Thomas Glave
ISBN: 9781845230982; pp. 220; May 2009; £8.99

This brave and remarkable novel, set in London at the end of the 1950s, and published in 1960, catches its 'brown' Jamaican narrator on the cusp between black and white, between exiled Jamaican and an incipient black Londoner, and between heterosexual and homosexual desires.

Denis Williams
Other Leopards
Introduction: Victor Ramraj
ISBN: 9781845230678; pp. 216; May 2009; £8.99

Lionel Froad is a Guyanese working on an archeological survey in the mythical Jokhara in the horn of Africa. There he hopes to rediscover the self he calls 'Lobo', his alter ego from 'ancestral times', which he thinks slumbers behind his cultivated mask. First published in 1963, this is one of the most important Caribbean novels of the past fifty years.

Denis Williams
The Third Temptation
Introduction: Victor Ramraj
ISBN: 9781845231163; pp. 108; May 2010; £8.99

A young man is killed in a traffic accident at a Welsh seaside resort. Around this incident, Williams, drawing inspiration from the *Nouveau Roman*, creates a reality that is both rich and problematic. Whilst he brings to the novel a Caribbean eye, Williams makes an important statement about refusing any restrictive boundaries for Caribbean fiction. The novel was first published in 1968.

Edgar Mittelholzer
A Morning at the Office
Introduction: Raymond Ramcharitar
ISBN: 978184523; pp. 215; May 2010; £8.99

First published in 1950, this is one of the Caribbean's foundational novels in its bold attempt to portray a whole society in miniature. A genial satire on human follies and the pretensions of colour and class, this novel brings several ingenious touches to its mode of narration.

Edgar Mittelholzer
Shadows Move Among Them
Introduction: Rupert Roopnaraine
ISBN: 9781845230913; pp. 352; May 2010; £10.99

In part a satire on the Eldoradean dream, in part an exploration of the possibilities of escape from the discontents of civilisation, Mittelholzer's 1951 novel of the Reverend Harmston's attempt to set up a utopian commune dedicated to 'Hard work, frank love and wholesome play' has some eerie 'pre-echoes' of the fate of Jonestown in 1979.

Edgar Mittelholzer
The Life and Death of Sylvia
Introduction: Juanita Cox
ISBN: 9781845231200; pp. 362; May 2010, £10.99

In 1930s' Georgetown, a young woman on her own is vulnerable prey, and when Sylvia Russell finds she cannot square her struggle for economic survival and her integrity, she hurtles towards a wilfully early death. Mittelholzer's novel of 1953 is a richly inward portrayal of a woman who finds inner salvation through the act of writing.

George Lamming
Of Age and Innocence
Introduction: Jeremy Poynting
ISBN: 9781845231453; pp. 320; January 2011; £11.99

This most insightful exploration of race and ethnicity in colonial and postcolonial societies reaches far beneath the surface of ethnic difference into the very heart of the processes of perception, communication and knowing. Tense and tragic in its denouement, this is one of the half dozen most important Caribbean novels of all time.

Elma Napier
A Flying Fish Whispered
Introduction: Evelyn O'Callaghan
ISBN: 9781845231026; pp. 248; September 2010; £9.99

With its feisty heroine and prose that sings, Napier's Dominican novel of 1938 is a major rediscovery, not least for its imaginative exploration of different kinds of Caribbeans, in particular the polarity between plot and plantation that is seen in a distinctly gendered way.

Austin C. Clarke
The Survivors of the Crossing
Introduction: Aaron Kamugisha
ISBN: 9781845231668; pp. 240; August 2011; £9.99

It is 1961 and a "Labour" party rules the self-governing colony of Barbados, but the sugar estate workers wonder whether slavery has ever ended. When Rufus, an illiterate canecutter tries to lead a revolt against the old order, he finds not only the colonial state but colonised minds standing against him.

.   Imminent

Wayne Brown, *On the Coast and Other Poems*
Una Marson, *Selected Poems*
Orlando Patterson, *The Children of Sisyphus*
V.S. Reid, *New Day*
Garth St. Omer, *A Room on the Hill*
Roger Mais, *The Hills Were Joyful Together*
George Campbell, *First Poems*

Titles thereafter include...

O.R. Dathorne, *The Scholar Man*
O.R. Dathorne, *Dumplings in the Soup*
Neville Dawes, *Interim*
Michael Gilkes, *Couvade/A Pleasant Career*
Wilson Harris, *The Sleepers of Roraima*
Wilson Harris, *Tumatumari*
Wilson Harris, *Ascent to Omai*
Wilson Harris, *The Age of the Rainmakers*
Marion Patrick Jones, *Panbeat*
Marion Patrick Jones, *Jouvert Morning*
George Lamming, *Water With Berries*
Roger Mais, *Black Lightning*
Edgar Mittelholzer, *Children of Kaywana*
Edgar Mittelholzer, *The Harrowing of Hubertus*
Edgar Mittelholzer, *Kaywana Blood*
Edgar Mittelholzer, *My Bones and My Flute*
Edgar Mittelholzer, *A Swarthy Boy*
Orlando Patterson, *An Absence of Ruins*
V.S. Reid, *The Leopard* (North America only)
Garth St. Omer, *Shades of Grey*
Andrew Salkey, *The Late Emancipation of Jerry Stover*
and more...